D0918828

Thought Criminal

Also by Michael Rectenwald from
New English Review Press:

Springtime for Snowflakes:
'Social Justice' and Its Postmodern Parentage (2018)

Google Archipelago:
The Digital Gulag and the Simulation of Freedom
(2019)

Beyond Woke (2020)

Thought Criminal

Michael Rectenwald

Published by New English Review Press
a subsidiary of World Encounter Institute
PO Box 158397
Nashville, Tennessee 37215
&
27 Old Gloucester Street
London, England, WC1N 3AX

Cover Art & Design by Ari Lankin based on his painting
Gripped, 18 x 30 inches, acrylic and oil on canvas.

ISBN: 978-1-943003-45-7

First Edition

NEW ENGLISH REVIEW PRESS
newenglishreview.org

Two kinds of symbol must surely be distinguished. The algebraic symbol comes naked into the world of mathematics and is clothed with value by its masters. A poetic symbol—like the Rose, for Love, in Guillaume de Lorris—comes trailing clouds of glory from the real world, clouds whose shape and colour largely determine and explain its poetic use. In an equation, x and y will do as well as a and b; but the Romance of the Rose could not, without loss, be re-written as the Romance of the Onion, and if a man did not see why, we could only send him back to the real world to study roses, onions, and love, all of them still untouched by poetry, still raw.

—C.S. Lewis and E.M. Tillyard, "The Personal Heresy: A Controversy" (1936)

Contents

CHAPTER ONE

Propagation Theory

C AYCE VARIN LAY IN BED rehearsing the sequence of
events that brought him to this pale-green motel room
in Angelus, Region of Kansas. Only a few months ago, as late as
March 22, he'd been a Distinguished Professor, holding presti-
gious appointments in Theory of Mind and AI-Neuroscience at
Transhuman University, Santa Cruz, Region of California. He'd
been a thriving research professor, a principal investigator. His
lab developed nano-interfaces for neocortex Collective-Mind
connectivity and employed numerous research scientists while
training several graduate research assistants. He appeared fre-
quently in Mediastry reports—often with Morgan Dickinson,
his colleague, collaborator, and friend. He sat on the Santa Cruz
Smart City Council, where he headed its Things and Agents of
Collective Mind (TACoMi) subsystem, overseeing the accelerated registration, mapping, and tracking of Significant Entities
within a 200-kilometer radius, as well as advanced data-shar-
ing with other Smart Cities. He also developed site-specific algorithms that predicted Significant Entity behavior within the
Smart City of Santa Cruz (SCSC).

At Trans U., however, he had not been sufficiently circum-
spect with a particular Graduate Research Assistant, namely,
Ginger Husserl, and TACoMi failed to predict her behavior, not
that it could.

9

She had betrayed his confidence. He lost his faculty and board positions, his wife Eve filed for divorce, and he was registered as a Thought Deviationist and Vaccine Resistor. His life as he knew it was over.

This morning, August 10th, at 1100 hours, he heard a beep from the motel room door and heard the door open from the outside.

"We're still in here ... trying to sleep!" he yelled across the room, thinking he was addressing a Service Robot entering to clean the room.

But the door continued opening anyway. Varin sat up.

Within seconds, a Robot Agent-25 stood beside the Mediastry Monitor a few meters from the foot of his bed.

"What are you doing in here?" Varin asked, seeing that it wasn't an SR.

The RA-25 stood silent, their eyes fixed on Varin.

"Arbeitern, what's going on in here?!" Varin yelled.

Arbeitern, Varin's Personal Robot Agent, had been sleeping. When they heard their name, they woke and assessed the situation.

"This is a Pandemos Federation Robot Police Agent."

"What are they doing here?!"

Arbeitern paused for a half second as he searched the data.

"You have been registered as a Banned Researcher. Your designation as a Banned Researcher triggered this event."

"Why didn't you tell me this sooner?!" Varin asked, his voice trembling.

"The registration took place at 10:55, 5 minutes before the entry of the RPA. The data became available to me at 11:00. It is now 11:02."

"My God! Can things get any worse?"

"Yes. But I cannot predict with certainty how much worse they can become before you die," Arbeitern answered.

"Of course not!"

The RPA spoke.

"We are Officer Botis, Robot Police of the Pandemos Federation, Western United State Division."

"Yes, what is this about?" Varin asked, alarmed and irritated.

"We are here to apprehend you. Please prepare to depart."

"Depart?! Depart for where?"

"We cannot answer that question at the present time," Officer Botis answered.

"What? Why not?!"

"We cannot answer that question either," Officer Botis answered.

Varin turned to his left as if to appeal to Arbeitern, but there was nothing Arbeitern could do.

Despite having been awake for an hour, Varin still hadn't fully grasped the significance of the encounter. Although he'd dreaded this fateful day for some time, he found it hard to believe that today was indeed that day. He soon realized that he had no choice but to comply, however. This RPA had the authority of the entire Federation behind them. And they now stood in his motel room and gazed at him indifferently.

Varin tried to delay the inevitable.

"Can I take a shower first?" he asked.

Officer Botis waited two seconds before replying.

"Yes," they answered.

Varin got out of bed and walked to the bathroom as Arbeitern and Officer Botis stood by. Wearing only underwear, he passed in front of Officer Botis sheepishly, and went into the bathroom. He undressed, turned on the shower, and stepped in. Once under the running water, and despite a wave of panic, he somehow felt vindicated that he was now under arrest. He must have been right about the virus after all. If he had been infected, an RPA wouldn't be here to arrest him, and not because they needed to avoid infection themselves—an RA presumably couldn't be infected by a biological virus. It was the uninfected that they wanted, he thought.

After a minute, Varin turned off the water, stepped out of the stall, grabbed a towel, and dried off. He wrapped the towel around his waist, traipsed past the Officer again, and walked across the room to his suitcase to get dressed.

Meanwhile, he noticed that Officer Botis's attention had lighted on the stack of paper laying on the nightstand. Varin had been creating paper on a 3-D printer to write *Propagation Theory* with a hand-held pin-point marker, obviously because it was more difficult for satellites and close-range sensors to read and digitize hand-written text than it was analog block text.

Before putting on his shoes, Varin went back to the other side of the bed and reached for the stack. But Botis's left arm extended and beat him to it, confiscating his book.

"They are interested in the papers," Arbeitern remarked.

"I can see that," Varin snapped.

"Do not forget your Q950 and gloves," Arbeitern cautioned, reminding Varin of rules that he knew all too well.

Arbeitern handed Varin the bubble mask and Varin slipped his head into it. Arbeitern then affixed the small oxygen tank to the belt of Varin's white jumper, connected the dangling hose from the tank to the bubble mask, and clipped the hose to the tape of the zipper. They then handed him a new pair of Urskin gloves, which Varin pulled on.

"Can my PRA come with us?" Varin asked Officer Botis.

Outpacing Officer Botis's reply, Arbeitern interjected.

"They will require that I accompany you, in fact."

"Yes," Officer Botis answered immediately after.

Slightly less panicked now, Varin studied Officer Botis for a moment. He'd never seen an RA-25 like them. They seemed to act deliberately mechanical and spoke in a stiff, automated cadence. They even moved in a herky-jerky manner. Their gray metallic head was almost perfectly round and made a whirring sound when it turned.

Varin whispered to Arbeitern.

"Why does Officer Botis seem so...*so...robotic*?"

Arbeitern answered at full volume, knowing that his response signified no additional jeopardy for Varin.

"Officer Botis is from an older series of the RA-25 model line, a limited series that ran for only six months. They were designed during an anti-humanist phase of Robotic engineering, when RA modeling after Human Biologicals was deemed *anthropocentric* and *robophobic.*" Arbeitern underscored these two antiquated terms. "The series was intentionally fabricated so as not to appear humanoid. An earlier series of RA-25s had eyes in the backs and sides of their heads. But this series made the Human Biologicals too uncomfortable and was soon discontinued."

Varin almost felt insulted that such a retrograde RA-25 had been sent to arrest him.

Now that Varin was prepared to leave, Officer Botis led him to the police car, and Arbeitern followed behind. Varin was blinded by the sunlight as it pierced through the transitioning Q950 that didn't darken fast enough for him. His pupils had been hyper-dilated. Officer Botis took the pilot's seat and Varin the passenger seat in front, while Arbeitern entered through the back door.

After a few turns on the side roads, the car soon bolted ahead on the straight and shimmering highway through Kansas, heading west. Officer Botis sat motionless behind the steering rod. The landscape presented little of interest to Varin, and Officer Botis apparently found nothing interesting about it either.

Detecting Varin's unease, Arbeitern spoke, as if acting the part of tour guide.

"Central and western Kansas consists largely of a repeating series of fields sown with hybrid crops, punctuated by older and newer silos. The newer silos are thought to be data warehouses disguised to look like grain depots."

Varin was distracted and anxious but he tried to listen so as not to think of anything else. He feared that Officer Botis, despite appearing outmoded, might be capable of harvesting his thoughts at such close range. But he couldn't help thinking about the virus and *Propagation Theory*. And he wondered what was in store.

"Now can you tell me where we're going?" he asked the Officer.

Taking advantage of Officer Botis's slow response time, Arbeitern interposed.

"Now that you have been secured in the police car, they will tell you where we are going."

"We are taking you to Essential Data, located in Data Area-48," the Officer replied.

"Essential Data is located outside of Sparks, Nevada," Arbeitern remarked.

"Why?" Varin asked the Officer.

"To cure you of the virus," they replied.

"I have the virus?"

"Yes, you have the virus," Officer Botis replied. "You resisted the vaccine."

"Then what's going to happen?"

"Good question," interjected Arbeitern.

"Thanks," Varin said sarcastically, turning toward the back.

"Then what's going to happen?" he repeated for Officer Botis.

"You asked a question as if you do not know the answer to the question. But you must know the answer to the question," replied Officer Botis.

"They think that you know the answer," Arbeitern said.

"But I don't know!" Varin yelled, as if to both the Officer and Arbeitern. He merely hoped to keep a conversation going.

"Do you not believe the Mediastry reports?" Officer Botis asked Varin routinely.

"Should I?" Varin asked.

"Things would have gone better for you if you had believed the reports. But it does not matter what you believe anymore," the Officer said.

Varin had a sinking feeling. Officer Botis's straightforward answer to his question alarmed him. Since they apparently saw no reason to hide this truth from him, he must have reached an ultimate impasse.

"What do the Mediastry reports say that I should have believed?" he asked the Officer. He wasn't really concerned about the reports. He knew very well what they said.

"You know what the reports say," the Officer answered.

"Please tell me anyway."

"The reports say that blood transfusions are the only way to cure the virus. The vaccine is the only way to prevent it," they answered.

"But why Essential Data? What does the virus have to do with data?"

"Why do you ask *us*?" Officer Botis replied. "We know that you have your own ideas about the virus, and data."

Arbeitern remained silent.

Varin was beginning to think that Officer Botis was a lot smarter than he seemed. This dumb robot act was just that.

Indeed, Varin had ideas about the virus and what it had to do with data. In *Propagation Theory*, he argued that the virus wasn't being treated at all. Rather, it was being propagated intentionally. The virus was actually a technology that connected the neurotransmitters of the neocortex to Collective Mind in order to conduct information flows between the two. Nanobots had been used to the same effect before, but the virus had proven more advantageous. It spread itself, and since it was supposedly biological and infectious, it didn't require consent. According to the Federation Mediastry, the virus had escaped a lab accidentally and *deterred* connectivity. It was also potentially deadly. The object was to avoid it at all costs. As such, the Federation required that all Human Biologicals receive the vaccine. Varin wrote that in fact the virus had been released deliberately, with the explicit aim of infecting as many Human Biologicals as possible in order to connect the neurons to Collective Mind and regulate the neocortex. The technology was aimed especially at Deviationists like himself. He hadn't quite worked out what the vaccine did, but he had some ideas.

The conversation stopped and Varin looked at the landscape around him. After a few hours, the plains gradually gave way to mountains, and soon mountains were complemented by desert. Arbeitern detailed the geological and the salient Human Biological history of the region, but Varin barely listened. The topology appeared alien, extraneous, and meaningless to him. They seemed to arrive at the entrance for Data Area-48 to the west of Sparks, Nevada, in no time, although it was almost dusk. A molten sun flared at the western lip of the desert sky and heat waves rose upward, swaying in slow motion above the desert floor. To the left of the highway, sixty enormous compounds spread across a 65-kilometer circumference. Each compound was a city unto itself, enclosing another sprawling giant. Officer Botis took control of the car as it approached the Area's core. After passing through the gates of nine circular fences, the three finally reached the center: Essential Data.

CHAPTER TWO

Essential Data

ESSENTIAL DATA LAY before them as they pulled into the driveway—a circular building with glass walls and a gray metal dome. It was built on a giant crater dug out of the desert floor. An inconspicuous blue LED sign spelled out the name on a placard in the bare lawn in front. The dome rose only twenty-five meters above the ground, but the circumference of the building was enormous. Faint blue and red blinking lights emanated from the data processors and passed through the light blue tinted glass walls.

Officer Botis parked the car, which immediately shut down. They got out and crossed to the open passenger door. Varin's seat swung out through the doorway above the ground. He slid off and stood beside the Officer on the pavement as the seat retracted. Arbeitern exited the car and stood beside them. Varin looked at the building before him. Although he'd never set foot in such a place, he knew most of what went on inside and now began guessing the rest.

"The Essential Data complex has a circumference of 1.65 kilometers," Arbeitern reported. "The Essential Data building houses the most important processors and data of Collective Mind. It has also become the primary site for treating obstinate cases of the virus."

"And this is where we must part ways," Officer Botis said. "I will escort you two to reception and leave."

"Did you hear the sadness in Officer Botis's voice?" Varin asked Arbeitern, whispering.

"Officer Botis cannot really care about you," Arbeitern answered at full volume. "RA-25s in their series cannot form attachments like Human Biologicals or other RAs. Officer Botis may have been programmed to sound sad when leaving an acquaintance. But their emotionality is merely a simulacrum."

This last suggestion disturbed Varin. He quickly tried to erase the thought from his mind and pondered his prospects. He reckoned that they wouldn't have brought him here just to kill or torture him. No, they either wanted to delete and replace what was in his neocortex or get something out of it. Or both.

Reception was just inside the nearest glass door. It was a spartan anteroom with gray walls and a high, concrete warehouse ceiling. A set of office chairs lined one wall, and a reception area lined the opposite one. An RA-30 entered from a door behind the reception desk, and looked at Officer Botis to dismiss him. Varin turned to watch Botis leave, and then turned back to the receptionist, who addressed Varin, and apparently Arbeitern as well.

"We are Kharon. We will take you through the steps of the process. We will come to check on you after each step of the process. Then we will introduce you to the next step, and so on. Do you have any questions?"

"Yes, I do," Varin answered. "What's the process? What are these steps, and how many steps are there?"

Arbeitern interposed. "The process is probably the treatment for the virus."

"Yes," said Kharon, responding to Arbeitern. "You don't know the process?" Kharon asked Varin. Kharon knew that Arbeitern had no access to the process data. Kharon's particular RA status granted them access to a specific partition of Collective Mind that included the process data, information about the patients who'd received it, their treatment, their outcomes, as well as other data, such as various explanations of the process. Kharon knew that most Human Biologicals had no such access either, but Kharon had learned to act as if they did.

Varin, meanwhile, acted like he had no idea at all about the process.

"No," Varin answered.

"The process is essentially a data exchange," Kharon said. "You have been infected by the virus and need to have the virus removed so that your thoughts can be corrected. The only way to remove the virus is by a blood transfusion; a special transfusion is the only sure way that we can rid you of the virus's harmful effects on the brain. Your thoughts must be corrected for normal brain functioning. To ensure a permanent correction, we must administer the vaccine after the transfusion. This will protect you against future infections and ensure continued normal functioning. Finally, we will determine whether or not the transfusion and the vaccine have been successfully administered. These are the first three steps of the process. If the transfusion and the vaccine are not successful, as many as nine additional steps may be necessary."

"This is a Bullshit Machine, right?" Varin whispered to Arbeitern. "They're spewing nothing but propaganda, right? Everything Kharon just said must be nearly the exact opposite of the truth."

But Arbeitern didn't answer him. Kharon was too close by and had overheard.

"We do not know how to answer these questions," Kharon replied.

"Never mind," said Varin, glad his questions had fallen on deaf RA ears. "I'm relieved. I'm finally being treated for the virus. I dislike incorrect thoughts as much as the next Human Biological and RA. And, as you can see, I surely don't want to infect anyone else." He smiled nervously and pointed to his Q950 as he spoke this last sentence.

Kharon was not impressed. "You may take that off now," Kharon said.

Arbeitern helped Varin out of the bubble mask and gathered the tank and hose together, holding them in one hand.

Varin went on. "May I get a sedative? How about Minuserall? Or whatever else you have? I'm anxious about this process and don't want to lose it here."

"We have to check on that," Kharon answered routinely. "Please have a seat."

Varin walked across the room and sat down, and Arbeitern followed. He refrained from saying anything to Arbeitern, but everything hinged on the sedative, he thought. If they didn't give it to him, he was finished. He remembered everything he stood to lose. He knew it meant the end of *Propagation Theory*, but wondered if it would include his entire knowledge base, other than the pedestrian elements common to everyone, which they no doubt wanted to preserve. He feared the loss of his identity. Without his own thinking, what would be left of him? It was not fear for his social classification, which couldn't be changed without the Identity Department's permission in any case. He feared the loss of his individual selfhood, or whatever it was that made him himself.

This reverie didn't last very long, however. Kharon seemed to have their answer about the sedative.

"Please return to the reception desk," Kharon called out through their loudspeaker.

"Yes?" Varin answered, as he quickly stepped to the counter. His eagerness felt ridiculous. Arbeitern followed him to the other side of the room.

"We have determined that there are no contraindications for the administration of Minuserall. However, we do not have access to Minuserall at this time. But we do have a related medication, known as Eraserall. Eraserall is in the same family as Minuserall. But it is slightly stronger. Would you like us to administer Eraserall?"

Varin knew a great deal about Eraserall. It was exactly what he wanted. He'd been taking it for some time now. And he knew the Mediastry ran ads for the medication constantly, although he tried to avoid Mediastry programming. He knew it underperformed and yet was overprescribed. It didn't do what it was supposed to do: erase your every care. It didn't erase your thoughts, either. It merely put them on hold. But it did something else. Varin believed it might be the real vaccine, which is why he asked for the related drug, Minuserall. He also knew that Eraserall was addictive. In fact, it was so addictive that you could become hooked from a single dose. Varin thought for months that he had a choice between taking Eraserall, dealing with addiction and its side effects, and losing everything he'd ever been or might become.

He swallowed the tiny pink pill and immediately felt its powerful properties. The effects were magnified after Kharon administered another, unknown pill. Kharon also explained that Arbeitern could not accompany him during the process. But Varin didn't care about having Arbeitern with him now. He didn't care about anything. His apprehensions about the process remained, but without any urgency attached to them. His head felt heavy and especially oblong. He had no concern about his identity and was not even sure what the concept even meant. Identity was just a lump of coagulated beliefs floating in a warm amnesiac pool, along with other notions.

After Varin became unconscious, Kharon wheeled him into the Process Room. When he woke, he found himself alone in a steel windowless chamber, seated on a heavy reclining chair, which looked to him like an old dental chair. His head was propped up slightly higher than his legs, and his arms and legs were strapped down just loosely enough so that he could move around a few inches, but not so loose that he could get up—although he had no impulse to get up. A round surgical light beamed in his face and the glare hurt his eyes. The Eraserall had hyper-dilated his pupils.

The surgical lamp dimmed and went out after several minutes. A string of small bulbs around the perimeter of the doorway emitted enough light to make the outlines of the room visible, although there was nothing in the room except for the chair, the lamp, and himself.

After a time, however, Varin saw a foggy shape emanating from the opposite wall—a long, undulating phosphorescent purple body growing in length and girth as it escaped the wall's bondage. He thought he might be hallucinating, but soon thought the purple body might be real. Ideas like these were not utterly uncommon, and Eraserall's effects contributed to their credibility. Some Thought Deviationists—including a growing body of physicists, cosmologists, and other Banned Researchers—had observed that some so-called spaceships, for example, didn't behave according to the constraints of physical laws. Many of these Banned Researchers had begun to use the term Extramaterials over Extraterrestrials, although they might have used either. Varin wondered whether this was an Extramaterial event of some sort.

Soon the wraith dissolved and Varin gazed at the wall for what felt like hours. The floodgates of his brain opened, and everything beyond him rushed in. He was at the full disposal of the environment. He slept like this, his mind an open wound through which anything might flow. He was feverish while the monsters had their way with the vesicle. He had no dreams. There was no organizing element—only a flourishing of chaos, as the outer space invaded an otherwise selective inner space. A deafening silence had a definite pitch, and characterless being had a peculiar character. The universe exhibited an intentionality—to what end wasn't clear.

A team of three RA-45s entered the room and woke him. He was now in a very mechanical state of mind. Everything had been boiled away except for facts. He was a prisoner. The three RAs looked more like aliens to him than they might have otherwise. Their heads were large plastic, lighted discs. Their arms and legs were made of sleek light metal and were tapered at the joints. Some fingers resembled blunted needles. Others were rubberized and as thick as his own. The strangeness of it all struck him suddenly.

"We are here to administer the vaccine," one of the three said. "Do you have any questions?"

He wondered why it took three such elaborate RAs to give him a shot as he was still strapped down, but he couldn't be bothered to ask.

"No," he answered.

"Wait just one minute," said another of the RAs. After

that minute, the third RA-45 approached him and extended a pin-pointed finger that pricked the sheath of his shoulder. Seconds later, the finger retracted. The other two RAs did the same in short order. The three RAs then left the chamber.

Varin slept again, this time for several hours. He woke when Kharon re-entered the chamber. They asked him, without much solicitude, if he wanted something to eat or drink. He had no appetite. His stomach felt hollow and inflated, as if pumped with air. He had an intravenous drip running into his left arm. Kharon handed him a cup of water, which he drank obediently. They then informed him that Step Three would be commencing in five minutes.

He thought about Ginger and what she might think, had she known what lengths the Federation had gone to deal with the likes of him. Would she believe this ordeal? If so, would she pity him? And, if she knew of it, would she fault him for it all?

At the appointed time, two Human Biologicals and an RA-50 entered the chamber. He felt rudely interrupted. One of the HBs spoke.

"Good morning, Mr. Varin. My name is Dr. Victor Fausten. I am an AI-Neuro-Virology physician recently assigned to Essential Data to deal with difficult cases of the virus. Joining us is our NAV associate, Dr. Molich, and our NAV assistant, Taylor. We will be asking you a battery of questions to see how the process has gone so far."

Varin disliked Fausten immediately. For one, he'd called himself doctor, but referred to Varin as mister. He wore a mindlessly permanent smile that verged on a smirk. He condescended when he spoke, putting an undue emphasis on each and every syllable. He was small-statured and fragile-looking, like a twig with a head. He appeared to be in his mid-to-late seventies, but he retained a baby face, as if he'd been pampered and protected from care his entire life. Molich, on the other hand, was a hale, thicker, and tall young man. He had freckles and bushy red hair. He was heavy-set and rugged, but reticent. He licked his lips incessantly, as if anticipating a meal. Both doctors wore white lab coats, and both had a light blue pod that looked like a bar of off-brand soap, only made of plastic, tucked away inside a side pocket of their coats. The pods were visible due to their weight that held the pockets open. The RA, Taylor, was very humanoid-looking. They had flesh-like skin that stretched over the smooth curves of their head, arms, hands, and neck. Varin assumed that the legs and chest were covered in skin as well, but they wore a white one-piece jump suit that covered their legs and torso. Their face was designed to manifest a pleasant demeanor. They even displayed a headful of thick dark brown hair that looked as real as either Fausten's or Molich's.

Fausten began the questioning.

"How are you feeling, Mr. Varin?"

"Sick."

"We are sorry to hear that, Mr. Varin. If it is any comfort to you, I will say that it is not atypical to feel rather disoriented after the first two steps of the process. You have undergone quite a procedure already. We administered a transfusion, then a serial and very powerful vaccine. The vaccine has a major impact. But we assure you that you should be feeling better in a matter of time, and if the treatment has worked, you will be free from the mental disturbances that brought you here." He paused. "What is your profession, sir?"

"Well, I was a Professor of Neuro-AI at Trans U., but I was fired. Now I write on my own."

"Why were you fired?"

"I had incorrect thinking. Or didn't I?"

"We cannot answer that definitively just yet. But it appears that the virus had corrupted your thinking. If you are like others who have had the virus, you certainly will have experienced various kinds of delusions, including paranoid delusions about the virus itself. As you probably know, the virus works on the neurotransmitters in the neocortex and has a way of altering the epigenetic programming—changing the culture genes, as it were—to malfunctioning culture genes, especially malfunctioning thoughts about the virus itself. Your neurological inputs have been blocked from the influx of the proper impulses from Collective Mind, leaving you to have all sorts of ideas, ideas that are erroneous, let alone unapproved. Have you had unusual thoughts about the virus, Mr. Varin?"

"I guess so."

"What thoughts have you entertained about the virus?"

"To tell you the truth, I can't even remember what they were. Fabulous ideas though, paranoid ideas, I guess. Whatever they were, I suppose they were incorrect. I do know they got me fired and labeled a Thought Deviationist, a Vaccine Resistor, and finally, a Banned Researcher."

"You mentioned that you write now. What have you been writing?" Fausten said this with a slight smile, as if he merely feigned an interest in Varin's writing.

"Don't you have my papers?" Varin asked. "Someone took them from me somewhere." He looked around, as if searching for the papers. "Anyway," he continued, "all I can remember is the title. Everything else is very foggy. After the title the rest of the pages are all blank—in my mind, that is. I'm sure the pages have something written on them, but I don't know what it is. The title was *Propagation Theory*, I believe, or something like that. I remember I was almost finished working on it, but I don't remember the content. Speaking of things that are missing, where is my PRA?"

"The RPA confiscated your papers, Mr. Varin," Fausten replied. At this, Fausten seemed to suggest that Varin had indeed been a criminal. "As for your Personal RA, we had to keep them out of the Process Room for security purposes. Now, back to your papers," he continued. "If your book was among the papers, then we have confiscated it. I have not seen it myself. Depending on how things go here, that may or may not be necessary." Fausten paused for a few seconds, suddenly appearing disturbed, perhaps by the possibility that he might actually have to read *Propagation Theory*.

"So, could you tell us what you think about the virus now?"

"Well, it's a nightmare, really, the virus is. But yes, I think the virus causes a terrible disease. It seems to affect the unvaccinated, causing them to have incorrect ideas about the virus itself, among other things. I've read and heard that it can also lead to death, but I haven't read or heard of anyone dying of it. A blood transfusion is the only remedy. And getting the vaccine is the only way to protect against future re-infections … Is that right?"

"That is correct," Fausten answered, apparently pleased. But as if correcting himself, his demeanor immediately returned to a cautionary smirk, and he continued. "But we need to scan your neocortex to make sure that you have been thoroughly cleared of incorrect thoughts … of the virus, I mean. We will apply these high-frequency, high-resolution encephalogram pods to your frontal lobe to search for traces of any remaining errant culture genes. That is, we are looking to see if you are still having delusions, if you are still infected." Fausten indicated that he referred to the blue pods that he and Molich now had in hand.

Just then Kharon re-entered the chamber. They wheeled a monitor, which they placed behind Varin's chair. Kharon remained in the chamber this time, Varin assumed to make sure that his incorrect thoughts had been properly purged. Fausten positioned himself on Varin's right side, and Molich on his left. They pressed their pods to Varin's temples and turned to the monitor for the reading. Varin felt the pods vibrate lightly. After thirty seconds, Fausten signaled to Molich, who removed his pod from Varin's left temple. Fausten then examined the right side of his frontal lobe by itself. The pod vibrated. After thirty seconds, he withdrew his pod and signaled to Molich again. Molich repositioned the pod on Varin's left temple. Both doctors studied the read-out as the pod vibrated.

Fausten walked around in front of Varin—his right hand rubbing his chin—and stood thinking. He addressed Kharon rather than Varin.

"Kharon, please release the straps and let Mr. Varin relax."

Varin tried not to show signs of relief. Was he being cleared and released, he wondered? Kharon unlocked the buckles and removed the straps. Varin stretched his arms and legs without giving any indication that he wanted to stand up and run.

CHAPTER THREE

Transhuman University

TRANSHUMAN UNIVERSITY was perched atop the Ben
Lomond Mountain ridge of the Santa Cruz Mountains,
overlooking the Pacific Ocean and the city of Santa Cruz. It had
once shared the majestic forests of a mountain campus with the
shrinking University of California. Like other typical universities, UC Santa Cruz's enrollment dwindled over decades and its
esteem declined with it. The received notion was that Collective
Mind had outmoded traditional higher education and made
knowledge acquisition a matter of instant package downloads.

But the deterioration of scholarship and knowledge was
more complicated and began long before Collective Mind and
direct downloads. Over many decades, several factors led to a
loss of faith in the possibility of Human Biological knowledge
altogether. Knowledge claims became increasingly tied to splin-
tering social identity categories. Tribal warfare, in which sheer
social and political power based on moral considerations alone,
such as which group had the *right* to be right, determined what
passed for knowledge. The relative social position of observers,
with those who had been historically subordinate claiming authority on the basis of their subordination alone, became the
sole criterion for the acceptance of beliefs. Subjectivism raged.
A growing obsession with social identity infiltrated every field.
Even in the science and technology fields, social identity be-

came the primary criterion for validity. In the end, a collective solipsism set in, resulting in epistemological nihilism. Eventually, the very objects of knowledge were called into question. This marked the end of Human Biological knowledge and the ascendance of the Transhuman.

Trans U. purchased half of the UC campus and soon sprawled across the rest, as building after UC building fell dormant. Trans U. would include some humanities and social science fields, but knowledge production and dissemination depended on an entirely different infrastructure. As with everything else, the human had been central in education, but it was superseded by the transhuman, both topically and methodologically. Knowledge once involved only Human Biologicals. Later, new knowledge agents would displace them. RAs would not only serve as information conduits and repositories, but increasingly as experimenters and analysts. In the past, universities had been attended. They later became growing partitions within Collective Mind. Like UC Santa Cruz, institutions that did not transform were outmoded and disappeared.

Ginger Husserl was a doctoral student in the departments of Theory of Mind and AI-Neuroscience at Trans U. In the Spring, she began writing her dissertation on the implications of brain interconnectivity and neocortex-Collective Mind interfaces for theories of mind. The working title was *One Brain, Many Minds; or Many Brains, One Mind?* Unlike the early philosophers of mind, however, and in accord with her contemporaries, Ginger E. Husserl wasn't interested in the mind-body problem per se, which was passé in any case. She assumed that mind and body shared the same material substance but exhibited distinct properties that couldn't be reduced to one another—any more than a landscape painting could be said to be a mere glob of acrylic paint. *Property dualism* and *emergent materialism* represented the correct theoretical configuration. The mind was an emergent property of matter and didn't exist independently of it. Yet, clearly, mind didn't behave like mere "dumb matter" either—although some Human Biologicals certainly did.

Like Edmund Husserl, professedly her ancestor, Ginger's

interests lay in phenomenology. She wanted to examine what became of the individual mind when the brain was connected to the databases and inputs of Collective Mind. She hoped to assess whether or not mental autonomy could be retained under hyper-connectivity, if it ever existed in the first place. If the mind was an emergent property of the brain and couldn't be equated with brain activity, she reasoned that it was possible that inter-brain connectivity and neocortex-Collective Mind interfacing did not spell the end of the individual mind as such. Connectivity might not amount to the sublation of individual mind—its incorporation and negation by the collective. If, on the other hand, the mind itself was harvested and subsumed in the process of interconnection, then individual minds ceased to exist. The key question was whether neural inputs and outputs determined brain activity alone, or overwrote the mind itself. In other words, could anyone have a mind of one's own in connection with Collective Mind? And, since it apparently depended on the self-conscious mind, individual identity for Human Biologicals was in question.

For Ginger, the issue had been especially personal. It touched on a high-voltage tension wire that had connected her and her previous mentor, the former Professor, Cayce Varin. She and Professor Varin had become very close collaborators. They spent many hours together working on white papers, sharing proposals, exchanging glances. They eventually became lovers. For her part, Ginger found it difficult to determine where he left off and she began. When he confided in her, explaining his otherwise secret views, she was terrified. It was already too late when she discovered that he had gone rogue, at least theoretically. Before she knew it, she had become involved with a covert Thought Deviationist. His arguments about Collective Mind and its threat to Human Biological self-determination alarmed her. When the virus struck and he eventually explained his theory, she found it to be very convincing and hid her mounting fears. What would become of her if she defected from acceptable opinion? What future would she have if she believed, with Cayce, that a malicious design underlay the order of things? In the hopes of resolving her own crisis, she decided to betray him. The revelation of their affair was used to seal his fate and protect her own.

But the dissertation drew Ginger to reconsider what Cayce had said, and her thesis trod dangerously close to heterodoxy. She even wondered whether apostasy had become inevitable. Her new dissertation director, Professor Yuēhàn Huang, was very leery of the direction she had taken and tried to redirect her into safer channels. Perhaps she could refocus to treat the increase of mental powers that Collective Mind made possible for the Human Biological mind, rather than the prospect of the latter's ultimate disappearance. Or perhaps she could examine collectivity and connectedness as a condition of mind in the first place. Did the autonomous mind even exist as such, not only now but even before the advent of Collective Mind connectivity? Wasn't the mind always already social? If so, nothing had been lost, while an enormous addition to Human Biological capability had been gained. If, however, she concluded that Collective Mind represented the end of preexisting individual HB minds, then the only reasonable response for those who cared would be to dismantle the former or accept, if such a word had any meaning, becoming mere drones. That conclusion would point to rebellion, most certainly a futile rebellion, against a vast and powerful knowledge infrastructure like none other in recorded history.

Eventually, Professor Huang and the other two members of Ginger's dissertation committee decided that Ginger's thesis was too dangerous and potentially too scandalous to allow. She could not write a dissertation that suggested that Human Biologicals might lose their identities as their minds were subsumed by Collective Mind. Mere days after she submitted a draft of her introduction to the committee, Huang wrote her a message:

Dear Ginger,

I'm afraid that the exploration you have begun is not viable. It risks exposing Trans U., the committee, and you to an investigation that could end with you being classified a Thought Deviationist and the committee members taken for accomplices, if not Thought Deviationists as well. The situation is particularly sensitive given the recent case and your association with it. We must avoid even the appearance of further indiscretion.

Please consider the alternative lines of argument that we have previously discussed. You may argue that the human mind has never been autonomous and therefore that nothing has been lost with Human Biological-Collective Mind connectivity or you may focus on the enhancement of the individual mind in connection with Collective Mind, or both.

I hope that you will agree that there is no threat to the Human Biological mind or identity as a result of the tremendous gains represented by Collective Mind. I know that I speak on behalf of the other committee members, Profs. Yang and Wu, when I say that we anxiously look forward to a resubmission of your thesis. Thank you.

Sincerely,
Yuēhàn

Ginger had anticipated a response like this but nevertheless was mildly shocked when it came. She knew that her line of reasoning was sound, her scholarship rigorous, and that the inquiry represented a perfectly legitimate intellectual endeavor. Her work's basis in established Theory of Mind and Neuro-AI was undeniable. Her introduction began with an extension of previous research and addressed a gap in the literature, a gap that she was quite astonished to find. Had no one asked these questions before? She could hardly believe it. But she was excited that no one had anticipated her. With the neuronal inputs increasingly supplied by Collective Mind, could the individual really be considered to have its own thoughts? If Collective Mind controlled the brain or at least imbued it with information as if generated by the subject's own brain, could one whose brain was thus directed be considered to have a mind? It wasn't enough to merely assert the social nature of all mental activity. The question was whether that sociality had become utterly determined by

Collective Mind. And, the other side of the coin was equally interesting. Would Collective Mind be the only mind extant, a mind generated in part by the brains of those connected to it? The fact that she could advance the question suggested that this was likely not the case, and she'd stated this clearly in the introduction. But she learned that she couldn't even ask the question. Although one of the alternatives Huang proposed did strike her as a possibility, indeed, one that she meant to explore, the committee considered it a settled question and a foregone conclusion that she was being compelled to reach in advance. The proscription against addressing the question appeared arbitrary and political rather than scientific or philosophical. Further, Huang's response provided an answer to the question about the possibility for independent thought. The answer was unequivocally No.

The virus had made an in-person meeting with the committee impossible. Meetings of more than two were now prohibited. She had no opportunity for a face-to-face discussion, where she might get a better reading on the committee's apparent absolutism.

Ginger lived on campus because her scholarship paid only for campus housing. When the virus struck, she couldn't afford an apartment on such short notice. She now paced her small glass and metal room in the Trans U. campus dorm, revisiting her relationship with Cayce. She found herself wanting to reach him, but then felt hopeless about any future communication. How could she locate him, and if she could, would he ever talk to her again?

CHAPTER FOUR

WeSpeak

GINGER WASN'T SURE that he would ever see it, but she sent Cayce a message on WeSpeak in early August. She figured that his account had probably been suspended or was being monitored. She feared that any message sent to him would be intercepted and that her Personal Accountability Rating, or PAR, would be damaged beyond repair. She might even be labeled a Thought Deviationist. Despite the risk, and the probability that he wouldn't receive the message, or if he did, that he wouldn't reply, she felt compelled to write it anyway. She created a sock puppet and texted Cayce at his usual account, refraining from using her name, or his:

> How could I ever have betrayed you? I was scared. I cared about you and was being drawn into your world and your ideas, and I panicked. I wanted to inoculate myself from scrutiny as well as my sense that I couldn't resist what you said. That's why I turned you in. I still care about you. Are you all right? Where have they taken you??? My Trans U. life is probably over. They rejected my thesis. I can't write what they insist that I write. I don't know what to do now. I need your advice about my career, and so much more. If you can find a way to forgive me, I'd be forever grateful and trustworthy.
>
> Your student, _____.

Ginger reclined on the off-white vinyl chaise lounge in her room, trying to calm down after sending the message. Already tiny, the room started to shrink around her. She felt claustro-phobic and sensed a panic attack coming on. She jumped to her feet, hurried to the bathroom, and opened the medicine cabi-net. Three bottles stared at her and she picked one up, checked the label, and put it down. The second one was it. She drew a cup of water from the faucet, removed two tablets, popped them into her mouth, and washed them down with the cup of barely cold water. Then she returned to the chaise lounge and laid back down. Within seconds, she felt better. The Eraserall worked.

Varin was cleared and released from Essential Data in mid-August. Kharon informed him that they labeled him vi-rus-free. An RA would drive him to his car in Kansas, they said. Kharon issued a data badge that allowed him to move around with relative freedom. "You will no longer set off alarms when you enter Smart Cities," they said. "The Thought Deviationist and Vaccine Resistor statuses have been removed from your profile, although you will remain a Banned Researcher, at least for now," they said. The latter designation, Kharon told him, meant that he could not engage in any kind of investigative writ-ing, at least until he had proven himself a trustworthy source. Of course, he thought, it would be impossible to prove himself a trustworthy source without first engaging in investigative writ-ing, which he was prohibited from doing. He was also forbidden to have his PRA, Arbeitern, until the Banned Researcher desig-nation was lifted. Varin was disheartened, but at least he could once again enter cities and wouldn't have to live in the middle of nowhere, traveling from cheap motel to cheap motel under the vain hope of eluding the sentinels of Collective Mind.

He'd stopped using electronic devices in April and relied strictly on Arbeitern for information, but Essential Data issued him a new Palm Reader 20.2 that attached to his left palm by Everlasting Adhesive, which allowed removal and reapplica-tion. Programmers at Essential Data even preset and person-alized the PR for him so that all of his apps and SRs were avail-able, along with most of the content. Of course, deviationist and questionable data had been deleted from the device, although it surely was retained by Collective Mind. He was still monitored, but no longer remained on Collective Mind's Close Watch List.

Varin was in no hurry to resume a connected life, however. Although his digital account was precariously low, he paid for another two nights in the same motel where Officer Botis had arrested him. He would need to have funds transferred to him at some point, he thought. But for now, he wouldn't worry. He took his time riding from Kansas to the West Coast, staring vacantly at the road most of the way, and stopping at rest stops and tourist sites, gazing around absently, without any real curiosity. He hadn't so much as glanced at the PR attached to his left hand until the third day after his release. When he finally did look, he activated WeSpeak and noticed a new message from an unidentified source. He tapped the icon and the Car Speaker read the message aloud. His first thought was that he was being set up. He hadn't the slightest reason to trust anyone, let alone Ginger, or someone posing as Ginger. He couldn't answer, he thought, and dictated a note to his wife instead:

> Eve, my nightmare is finally over. I'm in the clear, at least partially. I'm sorry for everything I've done and put you through, and how my disappearance must be affecting Angelina. I'm on my way back from the Midwest. Please allow me to come back, at least for a visit. I hope you can forgive me, but I understand if you can't.

But the Car Speaker notified him that his message was blocked. He tried calling but the call was immediately routed to voicemail, which meant that his number was blocked as well. Eve must have wanted nothing to do with him anymore. He wasn't surprised. He'd wrecked her life with Ginger, but even more so by defecting from acceptable opinion. He now felt remorse and regret for both. Why did he have an affair with a student? More importantly, why hadn't he just kept his deviationist thoughts to himself? Did he really need to speak his mind and make his unorthodox views known? When he'd confessed them to a student, he may as well have sent a so-called letter to the editor of the *Santa Cruz Future Times*.

Then, he tried to justify the disclosure to himself. As an educator, wasn't he duty-bound by a fidelity to legitimate and meaningful criticism? Didn't he have an obligation to be forthright with his students, especially his graduate students? In fact, shouldn't he have done even more, like write an op-ed, or give an interview to *The Mercurial*, the Trans U. student newspaper? What had become of the Global University System now that voicing dissident views was verboten?

It was no use. He had done himself in, and for no good reason. He'd blown up his career over something he could do nothing about in the first place.

He took over the car and pulled to the side of the road into a wide safety lane and parked. He wanted to study Ginger's message, or the message seemingly from Ginger. He tapped the icon and the Car Speaker read the note again. If this was really from Ginger, he should be careful, he reasoned. After all, she had acted ruthlessly in turning him in and now she apparently wanted to reconcile. Why? Had things gotten that bad for her at Trans U., he wondered? Then he pondered the last line of the text, which struck him as tacitly threatening: *If you can find a way to forgive me, I'd be forever grateful and trustworthy.* Was this just a slightly mistaken expression, or did it contain some kind of discreetly buried ultimatum: Either forgive me, or else I will not be grateful, or trustworthy? What more could she do to him, he wondered? Varin snuffed out the thought, assuring himself that he was being paranoid and catastrophic. After what he'd been through, he was easily alarmed by the slightest suggestion of menace. But he felt guilty about likely wrecking Ginger's life as well, so he decided to respond.

> If this is really you, I should apologize as well. I made a grave mistake by exposing you to my deviationist thoughts and I take it that you're apparently paying a price for them as well. As for advice, I'm afraid I don't know what to tell you, or what to do next, myself. This exile is like ejection from the Garden of Eden, only it isn't Eden at all, except maybe for those who don't know any better. The choice is between a

false paradise and a punishment without remission. I understand why you chose the former: you feared the latter. Now it seems that you really had no choice. I suppose that is to a degree my doing, though I think there's more to it—something about you, for one. Don't think I forgive you only now that we apparently face similar prospects, a life of banishment and uncertainty, and for the same reason. I forgave you the minute I fell from grace and I understood your betrayal once I learned what banishment really means. The only thing to do is somehow to make a life from the ruins.

Your professor, _____.

Varin thought for several minutes, wondering whether to send the message. Would it get him taken back to Essential Data for another round of the process? After all, Collective Mind would easily understand the context and thus the import of his reply. But it might miss its significance given the emotional content. He could only hope that the meaning was all too human to trigger a response. But did he really want to be so conciliatory? Her apology might have come from desperation rather than concern. On the other hand, what did he have to lose? What use was his newly granted permission without any hope for a future, any kind of future?

He sent the text.

When she'd gotten nothing back after so many days, Ginger gave up on receiving a reply. She tried writing a new introduction to the dissertation but couldn't complete so much as a single cogent page, and even the one paragraph she did manage to write struck her as an abject failure. The recent alienation from her studies, and the emptying of the campus due to the virus, reduced her world to a navel-sized pit. Since the scandal, she'd been shunned by fellow students and everyone but her dissertation director. Even he had been cool and cautious with her. She was certain that the other two committee members refused to address her at all. Things had only gotten worse since submitting her introduction and receiving the short reply. She now heard from no one.

She began to think of suicide and considered the possible

means of accomplishing it. She mulled over her options for days while she morbidly watched the endless Mediastry reports on the virus. One method was to down the bottle of Eraserall with a bottle of whiskey. She never drank, so this method suggested itself as having a good chance of succeeding. Another possibility was to jump from the rocks of Davenport Beach into the Pacific Ocean. Yet another was to step in front of a speeding car on Route 1. This option struck her as likely too painful, so she dismissed it. Finally, she decided. She'd go to Davenport Beach, take the bottle of Eraserall, drown it with a bottle of whiskey, then jump from the rocks into the ocean. She would execute the plan this evening and leave at 1900 hours. It was then, just before the appointed time of departure, that she received the notification from WeSpeak.

CHAPTER FIVE

Eraserall

C AYCE VARIN AND GINGER HUSSERL planned to rendezvous at their favorite spot—the bottom of a winding set of steps that led from Highway 1 down to New Brighton Beach in Capitola, Region of California, just outside of Santa Cruz. Since the onset of the virus, an order from the Governor of the Region of California made sitting or standing on dry beach sand illegal. It was still legal to sit or stand on the wet sand, but of course it was impossible to reach wet sand without first passing through dry sand, so beachgoing was effectively banned. New Brighton Beach, however, had the advantage of being partially obscured by a grass- and tree-covered cliff that hung like a shelf over the beach's furthest edge. The plan was to meet beneath the shelf and hopefully remain hidden. Varin would not leave his car in the beach lot, which would tip off the RPAs, but rather a few hundred meters up the road, in the lot of a restaurant that would be closed due to virus response measures. Ginger would travel by a driverless car so that no third party would know of her arrival at the forbidden beach in advance—nobody but the ItDrives system itself, that is.

Varin rode from Kansas to California without sleeping. By the time he reached the CA border in the early morning hours, he began hallucinating. He saw a giant truck lying horizontally across the highway that he'd surely run into unless he slammed on the brakes at once, which he resisted doing. He saw a small fleet of police cars in the rearview mirror and then one police car beside him in the left lane. He saw a pack of coyotes running chaotically into the highway and scrambling as the car approached. If he had been driving the car, he surely would have pulled over, but he wasn't driving the car, so he more or less enjoyed the theater.

Since receiving Cayce's text, Ginger's outlook changed considerably. Her suicidal ideation went into remission, and she even began to consider rewriting the dissertation, regardless of the committee's rejection of her plan. She might publish it as a book instead. Life beyond Trans U. could be possible, she thought. But she decided she wouldn't begin anything until she reconnected with Cayce. Their meeting was set for noon. At 11:30, she put on her bubble mask and attached the hose and oxygen tank, then tapped the ItDrives app to arrange for a car.

After finally sleeping for five hours at a rest stop, Varin approached San Jose by 11:25. He wanted to assert some control over the car, and, for the first time in as long as he could remember, he enjoyed commandeering a vehicle. Highway 17 stretched out before him, an open road with no cars or trucks in sight for kilometers, thanks to the virus response. Despite the car's active monitoring and reporting its own speed to the San Jose Smart City databases, he sped along at 175 kph, well over the speed limit. No RPAs were in sight and even if he was automatically data-tagged, his account wouldn't be debited because the funds would have been insufficient to cover the fine. It was a Safe Account that didn't overdraw but merely returned any charges over the balance. No matter how thick the Data Net became, he thought, minor loopholes could always be found and exploited. It was as if no system, however elaborate and thorough, could ever be completely closed.

Ginger's car arrived at the top of the steps above New Brighton Beach at 11:50. She got out, and instead of descending the winding steps, she walked along Highway 1. The road and its alleys were vacant except for small flocks of birds chirping and diving between trees on either side of the highway. The road bent and curved, and she walked along for nearly a kilometer, feeling like the last Human Biological on the face of the Earth. For the first time in many months, if not years, she relished the sun beaming on her bare arms, the back of her neck, and face. Not even Collective Mind could prevent her from experiencing, however faintly, these few moments of joy, although expressing that joy would have been vain in the absence of another Human Biological. She turned around and hurried back. She'd been a half hour and now was panicked that she might miss Cayce at the bottom of the steps.

But Varin was late in arriving anyway. After speeding past San Jose, he slowed down as he entered Santa Cruz. The once-familiar sites now appeared strange, almost as if he'd never seen them before but more so because he had, and they weren't the same. A hostility emanated from the streets, stores, and houses. They reproached him for something he'd done. He felt guilty. He'd committed an unforgivable wrong. The asphalt, the concrete, the bricks and mortar, the painted cottages, the brightly colored porch awnings, the lawns and sidewalks, and the mountains above—they all stood by implacably and testified against him. He was a wrongdoer. Yes, he was blameworthy for infidelity, but there was more. The town cried out its own innocence against his reprobate being.

Varin pulled into the lot of the Paradise Beach Grille, and before turning to the steps to descend, he noticed a solitary figure on the edge of the highway to the north. It seemed to be standing still, flagging in the wind and blurred by the moist sea air suffused by sunlight. He kept his eyes on this figure, which soon appeared to be coming closer. At a hundred meters, he recognized the gait and stature as Ginger's. Had she walked here, he wondered? Something about her was different. She seemed to have broken away and become an isolate floating at sea, a piece of bark or a single plank from a boat that had been shipwrecked, leaving the remainder to continue on by itself after the ship had gone under. She was a whole apart, rather than a member of an aggregate as before. She was saturated with sad resignation mixed with resolute independence. Finally, he saw her hair and face in relief against the deserted background. Her strawberry blond hair was tossed, her face buffeted by the wind. She had taken off the bubble mask and held it to her side. As her expression became visible at fifty meters, Varin noticed that she'd been crying.

Cayce had removed his bubble mask as well and left it in the car with his Palm Reader. Ginger noticed his wispy blond hair, which had grown longer and looked wild. His clothes were disheveled, and he looked like a castaway. His appearance caused her to burst into tears once more. She walked even faster and, as she got very close, she stretched out her right hand as if to shake his, but Cayce ignored it and stretched his arms, reaching around her waist and drawing her to his body. Their embrace was at once criminal and consecrated.

No words were spoken for minutes. Then they broke away and he motioned toward his car, asking Ginger to leave her PR inside. He walked to the cement steps as she followed. They said nothing until they reached the beach at the bottom. Cayce sat down on the dry sand and pulled her by the hand beside him. He began.

"I noticed that you've just been crying."

"Yes," she said.

"I'm sorry to hear of your troubles with the dissertation committee."

"Thank you, but I wasn't crying about that."

"What is it then?" he asked.

"I was crying because I realized that I've lost everything I ever wanted but recovered myself in the process. I was crying for joy."

"You feel relieved in some sense then?" Cayce asked.

"Yes, but also lost, yet somehow not terribly afraid."

"It's a strange feeling, an ambiguous sense when you come clean with yourself, isn't it?" Cayce said. "When you've let yourself fall, with a certainty that you will not die, but not at all sure what you're trusting to catch you. It's almost as if you come to believe in something greater than the world itself. And it looks totally crazy to everyone else."

"Yes," Ginger answered, amazed at how synchronized they were. "It's like jumping off a cliff without a visible net below, but feeling sure that you'll be caught and won't splatter on the rocks or drown in the ocean below." She thought just then of her suicidal fantasies, although this wasn't the same.

"I know that feeling very well," he said.

"Well, you got there first."

"Maybe, but it doesn't matter. Because it's like stepping out of time, too."

"It is. So, what are we going to do outside of time?" She didn't mean to mock him, but thought she might have sounded like she had. He didn't hear it that way, in any case.

"Well, I'm glad that I studied more than AI and neurology before graduate school," Cayce said, "and that I didn't merely download packets but instead actually read and thought about what I read."

"What do you mean?"

"I mean I have ideas about our subversion that come from literature, from myth, from history, from religion even. That may have been the source of my eventual undoing, in fact. There's nothing I can do about it now. I didn't properly prepare for a life without thought, as it were. But it provides some sense for what to think about our predicament."

"Oh, what ideas come to mind? I really want to know," Ginger responded. She said this realizing that she sounded as if she were clinging to his every word, but she actually had a detached sense of curiosity for a minute.

"For example," he said, "our situation reminds me of Voltaire's *Candide*, the eighteenth-century comical novel that ends with Candide saying after going through the Inquisition, being robbed, having his lover lose half her ass to a swordsman, thinking his ridiculous mentor has been killed only to reunite with him later…he says, 'we must cultivate our garden.' That's it. That's what he comes to and it makes perfect sense. What he means is that there isn't any prospect for changing the world at large, of convincing anyone of anything, of ridding it of evil, or of overcoming the enemy. All we can do is to build a small world of our own, an alternative to the larger world yet not against it. Just separate. It won't be a utopia, but it won't be hell either."

"What then?"

"A parallel processing system if you will."

"I meant, what will *we do* then, but I see what you meant. And you're right. That seems to be our only choice."

"It's not really, though." Varin said, hurriedly correcting her. He didn't want to be responsible for a complete defection when one wasn't necessarily determined, for her at least. "We could pretend to be revolutionaries," he continued, "and charge at windmills, struggling heroically and in vain, resigning ourselves to sure defeat but a noble cause nonetheless, or all the more. Fit for a movie in our own minds. Or, we could pretend to believe. You could acquiesce to the dissertation committee's demands, whatever they are—and we need to talk about that. You could banish deviationist ideas or pretend they don't exist in your mind, and so on. As for me, there's no going back. Well, I guess I could shine robots, or do some piecemeal programming for companies that know nothing about my history—and Collective Mind won't prevent them from hiring me as long as I don't do anything theoretical or major. Or companies that know and don't care, as long as I don't deviate again, at least publicly. It would be inglorious, humiliating, and I'd barely eke out a living. But you can still turn back, write the dissertation they want, become an assistant professor, turn out acceptable articles, develop some software of use to Collective Mind, and so forth. So, if you really don't want this fate, this garden, you don't have to accept it. I don't have to either, but my options are fewer and far less attractive. I'm an *ex-con*. You're a young grad student who can make it all look like a slight veering off the track, thanks to an errant professor, a bit of confusion that Collective Mind has rectified. It really is possible, but you'd have to recant more forcefully, express inordinate regret, be a good robot...Wait, I shouldn't have said that. I should've said you could be a useful member of Collective Mind—respectable, comfortable, and esteemed."

"I don't know if I can do that. I mean I can't simply delete my thoughts or forget that I've had them." She said this force-fully, as if correcting him. "And they didn't all come from you, so you don't have to feel responsible…or take all the credit for them either." She said this last bit teasingly, but sincerely. "Also, I really sense that there's an alternative, a robust alternative, one that more closely represents my calling, or if that is too lofty for you, that allows expression of my most…prominent talents and abilities, and also that doesn't conflict with…my mind, I guess it is. That's the best word I can find for it."

"Well, there's the Husserl in you!" Cayce joked, but meant it.

"I have to tell you something, something that may change your mind about me," she said. "Before I got notification of your text, I was about to kill myself."

At that, Varin felt rebuked and grew somber.

"I'm so sorry," he said.

"There's no need to feel sorry."

"I didn't mean to joke about what you're facing, or to di-minish it. It's every bit as daunting as what I'm facing. If it's not the same, that's only because you're younger and haven't…never mind. It's every bit as daunting if not more so because you're younger."

"When I didn't hear back from you for weeks, I figured you would never forgive me or that my message was intercepted, or that you were dead, or had become…I don't know. And so, I planned to take a bottle of Eraserall, wash it down with a bottle of whiskey, then jump off the cliff at Davenport Beach into the ocean, and drown."

"Thank God you didn't! What stopped you?!"

"Your message."

Varin looked at Ginger closely. Her hair blew across her lightly freckled face and she kept pushing it back, over and over. Raw intelligence beamed from her hazel-green eyes. Sadness seemed so out of place for such a wonder. What a waste of godly nature her destruction would have been, he thought.

"What became of you all these months?" Ginger asked after moments. "What did they do to you?"

"Well, I don't know exactly what they did to me. I only know what they said they did to me. You can imagine. I have a guess about what they actually did. But after traveling from motel to motel in the Midwest to avoid Smart City detection, I was finally picked up and hauled off to the main data center in Nevada, Essential Data, and was told I was being treated for the virus and given the vaccine, then checked for whether the treatment was successful. But I asked for an Eraserall before the process, as they called the treatment, because I suspect it actually works as a vaccine for the virus and I suspected they were actually administering the virus rather than treating me for it. I can't be sure. Actually, I thought that Eraserall had inoculated me to that point, but I didn't want to ask for that in case they knew about it, so I actually asked for Minuserall. I thought maybe Minuserall would work as well, but they ended up giving me an Eraserall. I could hardly believe it. If they administered the virus as I suspect they did, then the Eraserall worked, because if I'm right about the virus, I didn't have it then and I don't have it now. And if I'm right about the process, they tried to infect me with it. They told me they'd given me a blood transfusion, but I can only find one mark on my arm, where they inserted an IV drip, nothing but saline water, I think."

"Wait, you think Eraserall works as a vaccine against the virus?" Ginger asked, astonished.

"Yes, I've been taking it for months, and I'm dependent on it, though I only take it as prescribed, one per day...You said you'd planned to take a bottle of Eraserall. So, you're on it too?"

"Yes!" Ginger replied. "I've been taking it for a year! I've tried to get off it, but I can't. I have severe panic attacks and then go into a terrible withdrawal."

"We're both dependent on it. And that corroborates my theory. Eraserall is effectively a vaccine against the virus."

Varin thought he heard something coming down the steps as he was talking. It sounded mechanical. Three robot dogs bolted toward them, barking and snarling. After seconds, one of the dogs spoke in a deep full-throated voice that sounded like three voices or more:

"By order of the Governor of the California Region, it is

illegal to be sitting on dry sand. You must leave the beach area immediately!"

CHAPTER SIX

The Mediastry

VARIN AND GINGER LEFT the beach in Varin's car and headed to the Trans U. campus. Since they'd already been seen together by the robot dogs, they reasoned that they risked nothing more by continued contact. If their reunion had been prohibited, they figured, they'd already be in custody. And they not only had unfinished business but also possible future plans to discuss.

Varin drove through deserted Santa Cruz, then took the back way up the eastern side of the mountain to avoid the guarded entrances. Ginger's dorm, Singularity Hall, lay at the far end of campus in a forested ravine connected to the rest of the compound by wooden bridges that spanned gullies thick with small redwoods, evergreens, ferns, and moss-covered rocks. Since the onset of the virus, the campus had been almost entirely evacuated. Ginger was one of three or four student residents left in Singularity Hall and one of twenty or so students still on campus. The RA-20s, however, remained at their posts, guarding the dorms and the other campus buildings. RA-75s continued to conduct research and to report results to the Principal Investigators that headed their projects.

Although he was not necessarily a persona non grata, given his firing and Banned Researcher status, Cayce would be recognized and might be stopped. The problem would be ushering

48

him past the RA-20 at the back entry to the dorm. Under Ginger's direction, Cayce parked in the lot closest to the backdoor. Remembering to leave their PRs in the car, the two proceeded to attempt entry with no little trepidation. Yet, as they walked through the glass door into the building, Ginger noted that the RA was missing from their post. The pair rushed to an elevator and took it to the fifth floor without being seen, then scurried to Ginger's door.

Before they entered, Cayce said quietly: "We need to talk very softly when saying anything deviationist or the slightest bit questionable, so your Mediastry Monitor or other devices don't pick anything up."

"Of course," Ginger replied softly.

When they entered Ginger's room, a sadness came over Cayce. He felt badly that he'd interfered with a grad student's humble life. Ginger's pride in welcoming him to her dwelling only compounded the feeling.

After they removed their bubbled masks and gear, Ginger asked if he wanted to watch the Mediastry. On the way from the beach, Cayce mentioned that he hadn't watched Mediastry programming for months. He was relieved at Ginger's suggestion. He wanted to be distracted from whatever he was feeling.

"I guess I better get caught up on the reports about the virus," he said.

"Good idea," Ginger answered.

She switched on the Mediastry Monitor and offered him the chaise lounge.

"No, please, I can't take your chair," Cayce said apologetically, moving the chair toward Ginger.

"Nonsense," Ginger answered. "I'm perfectly comfortable here." She was already sitting at the foot of her bed. Cayce brought the chair beside her. His curiosity about the Mediastry reports overrode any inclination he had to say more.

As programmed by Ginger, barring major breaking news, the Mediastry reports began where her viewing had left off. Now, Robot Reporting Agents delivered accounts on the state of affairs in various regions of the Federation, beginning with the

United State. In a press conference, Washington, D.C. Mayor Wang Xiu Ying reported "an additional 500,000 new confirmed cases of the virus in the Washington, D.C., area. As usual, the infected, as well as the exposed, have been moved into isolation centers—in Alexandria, Arlington, Baltimore, Bethesda, College Park, Rockville, Silver Springs, Tyson's Corner, and other sites. Hundreds of Vaccine Resistors, meanwhile, are being taken into custody and treated in hospitals and emergency centers around the region."

The series on the virus included a report on the 290 million infected worldwide, the 750 million unvaccinated, and the 500 million infected and exposed being held in isolation centers around the Federation, including in the Regions of Germany, Russia, China, and the United State.

After the twenty-five-minute report on the virus, a local news item aired. To Cayce's astonishment, it was about Morgan Dickinson, his former colleague and co-author.

"Morgan Dickinson has been a prominent research faculty member at Transhuman University for almost nine years. In early May, he was admitted into a treatment center in Malibu and diagnosed with Substance Intake Disorder. He was relieved of his position, but remains eligible to return upon completion of the Substance Intake Disorder Treatment and other protocols," the RRA stated.

Although Ginger knew about this, she hadn't told Cayce. It hadn't seemed important. But this was only the background for the current report. The real story was that Dickinson had just confessed to Thought Deviationism and Vaccine Resistance. Further, the RRA stated, "Dickinson has corroborated the charges of a graduate student at Transhuman University, 26-year-old Ginger E. Husserl. Husserl reported in March that her professor, Cayce Varin, admitted to deviationist tendencies and Vaccine Resistance. Now, Varin's former colleague is backing Husserl's claims."

In a clip, Dickinson was shown denouncing his coauthor and former confidant.

"I don't trust Cayce Varin, and I don't think Collective Mind should trust him either. I think he's managed to bamboozle the staff at Essential Data and that he still has the virus and remains a covert Thought Deviationist. At the very least," Dickinson went on vehemently, "Cayce Varin should be watched closely and should remain a Banned Researcher, indefinitely."

Cayce suddenly panicked and was unable to speak or think for minutes. Thoughts then followed, and he turned to Ginger and managed to articulate a coherent statement.

"I know what is going on here," he said, turning to Ginger, his words sounding all the more desperate for being whispered. "Dickinson's turned informant to get his job back. He's sacrificing me—me, an already wounded former colleague and friend—to appease the stewards of Collective Mind...Or is he speaking for, or as, Collective Mind?"

"I wonder what drug he was on," Ginger whispered back. "Whatever it was, he's supposedly off it now. But he sure sounds like he's still on something!"

"Oh my!" Cayce responded, almost under his breath.

"What?" Ginger pleaded.

"It had to be Eraserall! He had to be on Eraserall! That would account for his...wait, I never told you. Dickinson was a covert Thought Deviationist and Vaccine Skeptic. Well, you already know that now. The Mediastry report is accurate on that score, on one thing, for once. They always mix a little truth with lies, just enough to retain a shred of credibility...But not too much. It's necessary that HBs become ardent believers in lies. Adherence to nonsense demonstrates more loyalty than acknowledgements of the truth. Anyone can affirm the truth. Only true believers faithfully affirm nonsense. But he and I shared our views and agreed on just about every point. Discussions with him even helped me develop my ideas for *Propagation Theory.*"

"So now he says he's off the drug and free of the virus, which means he is off the drug but has the virus, right?" Ginger asked.

"That would be correct," Cayce answered. "He no longer takes the real vaccine, Eraserall, so he's now infected. His neurons are now connected to Collective Mind. The virus is providing direct, real-time monitoring and control of signals to and from the neurons in his neocortex. So, who knows what's left of his own thoughts and motivations, if anything? He sure sounds like he has an axe to grind. But it could all be an act. He may be nothing more than a ventriloquist's dummy at this point. But whoever or whatever is in charge of his thoughts, they sure are throwing me under the bus, as if I am not already a dead man."

At this, Cayce almost winced, realizing that he'd inadvertently recalled Ginger's betrayal.

"Do you think your status is going to change again, thanks to this report?" Ginger asked.

"I have no idea. It's not good, that's for sure. But I wouldn't be the least bit surprised if an RPA picked me up in a matter of minutes…But, for you this could be good," Cayce went on. "Dickinson's corroboration rehabilitates you to a degree. And, it also makes you out to be a victim. Having a victim status is always good."

Ginger ignored Cayce's last suggestion and wanted to talk about Eraserall.

"Tens of millions of Human Biologicals must be on Eraserall," she said. "So many people have anxiety. You can't tell me that every one of them is a Thought Deviationist. Are that many people harboring secretly subversive ideas without ever spilling the beans? There's got to be more to it."

Cayce had thought about this before. He knew Eraserall was a necessary condition for Thought Deviationism. But it couldn't be a sufficient cause. There had to be something else, just as Ginger suggested. But what was it?

"Right," said Cayce, "not everyone on Eraserall is a Thought Deviationist. In fact, I would argue that a small minority of Eraserall users are Thought Deviationists. Yet every Thought Deviationist that I know of so far has also been an Eraserall user. So, another factor, or more likely several other factors, must be present to account for Thought Deviationism. Part of me wants to say that only people who know how to think and take Eraserall can become Thought Deviationists, but that sounds arrogant."

"I think it has to do with the level of skepticism about the

Mediastry," Ginger said. "Eraserall users who unquestionably believe the Mediastry would not be Thought Deviationists. Maybe the the virus isn't even necessary to keep most HBs in line with Collective Mind. Maybe the Mediastry takes care of that. So many who don't have the virus may as well have the virus. The Mediastry effectively infects them."

Ginger had hit the nail squarely on the head as far as Cayce was concerned.

"Amazing!" Cayce exclaimed. "The thing is," he continued, "we can't be reliant on Eraserall to keep us virus-free. It's inevitably going to be discovered by Collective Mind. Furthermore, it's addictive and we'll have to increase the dosage. And soon enough we'll need to undergo Substance Intake Disorder Treatment, and when we do, we'll be among the infected, and that will be the end of us. I mean that will be the end of whatever thoughts are our own, I think. I won't be me, and you won't be you, and so on."

"So, we need to isolate the property that just so happens to inoculate us," Ginger said.

"Exactly! Then we need to reverse-engineer the inoculating property and produce it ourselves."

"How are we going to do that?"

"Well, first of all, we need a chemist, a really good chemist. Someone who's also been taking Eraserall. A chemist who's also a Thought Deviationist. Someone we can trust. Then after this deviationist chemist locates the property, we can make a replacement medication and more or less mass-produce it, using 3-D printing. We also need to make sure the new med isn't addictive. We don't want to have to seek Substance Intake Disorder Treatment for the new med after all that trouble."

"Right. But we can't advertise for a chemist who's also a Thought Deviationist."

"Naturally. We need to find them through the network."

"What network?"

"The network of Thought Deviationists."

"I didn't know such a network existed."

"You wouldn't. I didn't either, until I was outed. Then Deviationists came to me."

"How?"

"There are smart people among us, Ginger," Cayce answered. "They've created a new encrypted communication system that even Collective Mind hasn't cracked. Not yet, at least. Hopefully not yet. I've been out of the loop for almost a week now. And the network only started forming about a week before I was contacted."

"Are there names for this network and the encrypted system?"

"No," Cayce answered. "One thing about this network. They don't like using proper names for anything."

"Why not?"

"For one, when something is given a proper name, it becomes easier to locate. When a name is used enough, it gets picked up. Then it's just a matter of time before it's located and taken apart. Then everyone using it is also located. And furthermore, Thought Deviationists don't like proper naming. A historian among us says turning everything into a proper name is one of the features of Collective Mind's totalizing procedures. It's one of the procedures of all totalizing systems. And this historian has convinced everyone that we should do everything we can to avoid creating a world like the one we're living in. Also, I can't give out any names to you. Not yet anyway. You have to be introduced first."

CHAPTER SEVEN

The Vaccine

VARIN AND GINGER HAD TO decide where to go. Staying in Ginger's dorm room was clearly not a viable option. They joked about the absurdity of an ex-professor moving into his ex-student's dorm room. But considered from a purely practical standpoint, the arrangement was untenable. Varin couldn't come and go from the dorm room and elude the RA-20s forever. Plus, the room and the bed were too small for two people. Ginger had decided to drop out of Trans U. anyway. After discussing the dissertation committee's response to her introduction with Cayce, she realized that the prospects for completing a dissertation the committee would accept were anything but promising. Moreover, she didn't want to participate in what she now saw as a charade.

They slept in the dorm room for a night. The next day, Cayce went to work on the matter of funds. How might he have funds transferred to his account, and from where? He remembered his retirement account. Could he liquidate it now that he no longer worked at Trans U.? A moment's search told him that he could. He was only 48, but his retirement package allowed for early withdrawal in case of dismissal. When he learned the amounts, he rolled the several accounts over into one fund, then downloaded the entirety into his bank account. He then transferred half the funds to his wife's personal bank account, leaving enough to live modestly for almost two years—if it came to that, and barring major emergencies.

The two then talked about where they might move and how they might live. Low population areas in the West and Midwest of the United State appeared optimal. For one, they might elude Smart City surveillance—not that they were official fugitives from Collective Mind, as far as they knew. But the less they encountered Smart Cities and officers of Collective Mind, especially RPAs, the better. They wanted to avoid the virus as well, if at all possible.

Considering their criteria for a new location—low cost of living, low population, and relative isolation—they eventually decided on Chloride, New Mexico. Not only was Chloride small and remote, the town also shared a name with an important chemical. It was the anion of Chlorine, an essential ion for neuronal signaling. Neuronal signaling was a mutual interest, and they were in immediate need of a chemist. This seemingly arbitrary and ultimate reason seemed as good as any other for choosing a place to live.

Chloride lay at the eastern edge of the Gila Forest, not too far from the Arizona line. The nearest major highway was Intrastate 25. They could catch I-25 from Intrastate 70 East, which lay to the south. They would head there that very day.

Ginger packed her things and they loaded the car. The pair bid a final goodbye to Transhuman University. While Ginger's departure was mostly a relief, Cayce was despondent. After all, he was not only leaving his former workplace, but more importantly, he was leaving the town where he'd lived with his wife and daughter, without any chance of seeing them, maybe ever again. He told himself that he'd return when things cleared. But he had little hope of that in the foreseeable future.

They set out for Chloride that afternoon. Only five hours long, the drive proved easy. As their PRs were on them in the car, they couldn't talk much or broach any topics that would lead to anything remotely deviationist. When they neared the town, they found temporary accommodations at the outlying Geronimo Trail Guest Ranch, situated in the southeast corner of the forest. The setting bore little evidence of contemporary developments, exactly as they'd hoped.

After ordering and eating dinner, Ginger and Cayce went right to work on questions about the virus and the vaccine. There were no monitors or other Smart Devices in the room, and they'd left their PRs in the car, so they could now speak openly and without whispering. They sat on the edges of their respective beds, facing each other. Cayce began.

"Let's assume that the virus consists of nanobots made from DNA. This would be consistent with other nanobot technology used for Collective Mind connectivity. So, what's new about these nanobots? What's new about the virus?"

"Well, for one, it's communicable," Ginger answered. "It spreads from HB to HB by some means."

"That's what I thought," said Cayce, putting his hands together as if to say, close, but not quite. "But now, I'm not so sure," he continued. "That would mean that the nanobots duplicate themselves and spread. But why would they be any different than other nanobot technologies? What I mean is, what would justify calling the nanobots a virus in this particular case? Even though Collective Mind could say anything about the nanobots, let's assume that there's something distinct about these nanobots that is reflected in the use of the term 'the Virus.' In other words, let's assume that the nanobots can actually reproduce and spread. I wonder why earlier nanobots weren't able to reproduce and spread."

"Maybe they were," Ginger said, challenging him.

"Maybe, but I have my doubts. If the virus is already communicable, why not merely let it spread on its own—after infecting numerous sub-population groups? No, I don't think that's it. I'm beginning to think that it's the vaccine that enables the virus to reproduce and spread. Otherwise why would the process be necessary?"

"How ironic would that be," Ginger said, leaping up inches from the bed, and sitting back down just as quickly. "A vaccine that not only doesn't stop the spread of a virus but actually spreads it!"

"Exactly!" Cayce exclaimed, pointing and drawing down his right index finger as if making a mark to chalk up a point on an imaginary scoreboard. "This is how twisted the Mediastry programming is. It propagates an explanation that's the precise opposite of the truth."

"Right, that would be consistent with my experience," said Ginger. "It's more likely true if in fact it seems inconceivable." She ended this statement with a sign of resignation and disgust, resonating as it did with her recent experience with the dissertation committee.

"But we're getting ahead of ourselves here," Cayce interjected, impatient not to let the conversation get derailed. "Let's hold off on that for now," he continued, correcting himself more than he did Ginger since he'd initiated the commentary that led off track. "Because I think there's more to the vaccine than that … It must do more than spread the virus. Otherwise, the virus would simply include the vaccine, or whatever reproduces and spreads it."

"All right," Ginger said, "and what might that something be?"

"Well, first, let's talk about the probable composition of the virus. And how it works. And to what ends. Then we may be able to figure out what the vaccine is and what it does to the virus. Because obviously the vaccine operates on the virus."

"OK," Ginger conceded.

"Good," Cayce said. "So, like earlier nanobots, the nanobots comprising 'the Virus' provide a gateway for the signals from Collective Mind. Likewise, they are gated, they're gates that open to receive and channel Collective Mind signals to the neurons, and they also translate the frequency of Collective Mind signals into the frequency of neuronal signals."

Cayce got up and went to the kitchenette to pour himself a glass of water. He was already feeling overheated.

"Right," Ginger said, raising her voice slightly, then waiting for him to sit back down. "And the virus probably includes electromagnetic nanoparticles that amplify the incoming and outgoing signals, or at least the incoming signals. Signals from

Collective Mind need to compete with and overwrite autogenerated signals."

"Yes. For sure. Excellent point…Now, leaving aside the obvious, that these nanobots have hooks that attach to the neurons and penetrate the cells, the question is, what relationship might the gates have to the vaccine, and vice versa?"

"These gates, how would they open and close?" Ginger asked.

"Well, the gates would open with exposure to heat and close when heat is reduced. Heat would expand them. Less heat would close them … And what causes heat in the neurons?" Cayce asked.

"Neuronal activity," Ginger answered.

"Right," Cayce said. "And, at the same time, the heat would also indicate neuronal activity by means of the opened gates."

"Why, what would that matter?" Ginger asked.

"Well, the vaccine could come into play here."

"How so?"

"Well, when neuronal activity is greater, the gates open wider…"

"Right," Ginger broke in. "Then what?"

"What if the open gates trigger the nanobots to send a signal to the vaccine?"

"So, the vaccine is notified by the virus, by the nanobots, when the gates open too wide?"

"Right!"

"And the gates open 'too wide,' when?" Ginger asked. "When autogenerated neuronal activity is 'excessive,'" she added, answering her own question.

"Precisely," Cayce responded.

"In other words, when the HB is thinking 'too much!'" Ginger said with excitement, lifting herself off the bed again and sitting back down.

"Yes!" said Cayce, almost yelling.

"Wait, don't tell me! Could the vaccine then send a signal, or multiple signals, to the virus … to interrupt the autogenerated neuronal activity?"

"Yes, indeed! So, the HB's autogenerated thoughts are effectively shut down and Collective Mind signals dominate," Cayce added.

"Speaking of ironies again. As it turns out, while Collective Mind connectivity is touted in the Mediastry as being 'open-minded' and 'progressive,' in fact, the mind is more 'open,' so to speak, when it is autogenerating neuronal activity, when the HB is thinking for itself," Ginger remarked.

"Good one," Cayce said. "So, it's not a retrograde Luddite perspective to prefer autogenerated neuronal activity after all."

"But why would only autogenerated activity open the gates 'too wide?'—as opposed to the signals from Collective Mind, I mean?"

"Collective Mind's signals must be cooler than autogenerated signals."

"Right, that makes sense."

"Of course, we are only speculating here," Cayce cautioned. "Unless we were able to get our hands on the actual specs, we are really only guessing. But this explanation does account for the virus, the vaccine, and the relationship between the two. It also explains what I underwent at Essential Data."

"Oh really, tell me," Ginger implored, eager to hear more about Cayce's trial.

"OK, if you insist…

"…In a windowless cell known as 'the Process Room,' Cayce obliged, "I was strapped down. After what felt like hours, I saw what must have been a purple gas discharged from the opposite wall. I had no idea what it was at the time. I was drugged. But this gas must have been a nanobot swarm, the virus. It was dispersed throughout the room, and I must have inhaled 'the Virus,' so to speak."

"Jesus. They're actually using gas chambers!" Ginger said with amazement and revulsion.

"Yeah, can you believe that? It's too outrageous to be believed. And for that reason, it's never considered possible."

"Right. But what then?"

"Well, you're not gonna believe this, but three of the most

bizarre-looking RAs entered the chamber. They looked like classical aliens. They had flat lighted heads that blinked when they talked.'"

"What did they do?"

"They injected me with something, one by one. This was 'the Vaccine' as such. So the vaccine must have three distinct elements to it."

"And nothing happened, right?"

"Well, nothing that I could tell. But then again, even if the process had taken, I might have felt nothing anyway. But I felt nothing. Then I fell asleep, until two HBs and an RA entered."

"Then what happened?"

"Step 3 of the Process: The head HB began questioning me to see if I still had any deviationist ideas. And I really had all the thoughts wiped out of my mind, so it was easy to pretend to be 'disinfected,' as it were—to be infected. To tell you the truth, I actually thought I might have been reprogrammed. I felt utterly vacant."

"That had to scare you."

"Not really. I didn't feel anything. And I didn't care."

"What did they ask?"

"The head HB asked me what I'd thought of the virus before, and what I thought of it now."

"What did you answer?"

"I couldn't even remember what I thought of the virus before and told them so. And I just spewed back the official line when asked what I thought now. I wasn't sure whether I believed what I was saying or not."

"And you didn't feel like you were acting?"

"No, I didn't."

"But what really happened is that the Eraserall, an actual vaccine, had blocked the attachment of the nanobots to your neurons. And because the nanobots never attached themselves to the neurons, the vaccine did nothing. Eraserall blocked the neuronal attachments, and thus the vaccine had no effect."

"Yes, but I didn't realize it until hours later. I noticed my thoughts returning only hours after I was released and was let out of there. But before that, they pressed these encephalograms to either side of my frontal lobe, to monitor my neuronal activity. Luckily, nothing showed up."

"Remarkable," Ginger said, admiringly. "You performed perfectly. You must have employed some serious thought control, without even knowing it."

"Apparently, yes."

They both relaxed a bit and leaned back on their hands. It was as if Cayce had undergone the process again. He was exhausted, as was Ginger, who felt like she'd gone through it herself.

After a few minutes, Ginger continued.

"I wonder how the vaccine spreads the virus then."

"I do too. Do you have any ideas?" He didn't have the energy to think of anything just now.

"Well, the vaccine must include RNA. It would have to. It must transmit RNA to the nanobots, which use it to self-replicate. So that's part 2 of the vaccine, part 1 being the gate monitoring system and part 3 being the system that shuts down autogenerated neuronal activity."

"Brilliant," Cayce responded, although without the force he might have exercised if he hadn't been so tired. "Then, given that the newly made excess of nanobots have no neurons to attach to, they're released, probably through respiration. I would imagine the replicated virus also travels as an aerosol, just as the mechanically induced version does, the one they tried to infect me with…" he trailed off.

"And when another HB comes within a certain distance, there's a transmission and infection," Ginger added.

"Yes," Cayce said, and paused momentarily.

"…So, we've just outlined a theory of the virus," he went on, "essentially revising and completing a sketch of *Propagation Theory*. We now have a working hypothesis that explains why 'the Virus' and 'the Vaccine' were introduced…With the vaccine, the virus reproduces and spreads by itself, unlike other nanobots, those used previously. Further, the virus acts in conjunction with the vaccine. The vaccine serves as a regulator of the nanobots comprising the virus. While earlier nanobots allowed for neocortex-Collective Mind connectivity, the vaccine ensures that signals from Collective Mind dominate the neuronal activity in the neocortex. That is, the vaccine ensures that Collective Mind dominates the 'thinking' of the Human Biological."

"So, there you have it," added Ginger, feeling satisfied.

Cayce felt satisfied too, although depleted. As importantly, he now felt confident about introducing Ginger to the network of Thought Deviationists.

With that, Ginger decided to go for a hike in the forest, while Cayce took a nap.

CHAPTER EIGHT

The Followers:
Agent Robots and Human Biologicals

VARIN WOKE WHILE Ginger was still out hiking. He decided to retrieve his PR from the car and began to run searches for his name in various Collective Mind databases. He found thousands of new entries from the last twenty-four hours alone—mostly about Morgan Dickinson's charges against him. He felt no surprise over these. But he found thousands of fake entries, titles without content, clearly derived from his personal and professional history, yet involving terms combined nonsensically. These blank entries had such titles as "Thought Deviationist Absconds with Girlfriend Smoking Eraserall Till Sexbot Wife Calls RPAs' Retirement Fund," "Vaccine Resistor Gives Up Sexbot for Transhuman University Virginal Excursion into Collective Mind Withdrawal," and "Eraserall Overdose Causes Arbeitern Death on Intrastate 25 Cabin Fever Fast Forward." These were but three of nearly endless, even more absurd, yet seemingly omniscient-sounding titles.

Collective Mind was connecting private and public elements of Varin's life into series of non sequiturs. If such entries about him had existed before, he hadn't noticed them. Records of his own searches were likely being used because he had searched for some of these terms many times, although not always together. Yet some elements that he hadn't searched for bothered him. He'd only thought of buying a sexbot during the period he spent alone with Arbeitern in the midwest, for example, but had never followed through. Why was this being thrown up as such? He had worried about Eraserall withdrawal in the event that Collective Mind denied him and Ginger future access to the drug, but he knew better than to search for Eraserall. The words "overdose," "excursion," "cabin fever" and "wife calls RPAs" were the most troubling. Clearly, his movements with Ginger were being tracked and his mind had been read, but how and to what end? And what about the last phrase? Had his wife called the RPAs after receiving funds from him, or had he merely worried, subconsciously, that she would? Most importantly, what was the source of these titles? Were they merely the excesses of Collective Mind activity thrown together randomly, or were they taunts—machine-generated, or even HB-machine-generated spamming—directed specifically at him?

When Ginger came back from the hike, she found Cayce in a frenzy. She was smiling until she noticed him pacing and rubbing his forehead.

"What's wrong?" she asked.

"I'm too upset to explain," he answered brusquely.

"What is it?"

"Nothing."

"Did you take your Eraserall today?" she asked leadingly.

"Yes. That's not it."

"What is it then?" She asked again.

"So many things. I'm too frustrated and alarmed to talk about it. Plus, my PR's right here." He held up his left hand to show her. "Not that it matters. It's not like hiding anything is possible anyway. Collective Mind knows what color underwear I'm wearing today for Christ's sake," he said sarcastically.

"What happened?" Ginger implored again.

"Just every detail of my life, private and public, being displayed on Collective Mind interfaces—an endless series of blank entries with ridiculous yet unnervingly detailed titles, that's all."

"Oh, I've seen those before. Don't worry, no one pays any

attention to them."

"I'm not worried about anyone paying attention to them. My reputation is hardly my concern anymore," he said bitterly. "I'm worried about what they indicate. Some included suggestions about us running off together to a cabin and withdrawing from Eraserall!"

"OK, but we're not doing anything wrong. We're not Thought Deviationists."

"Maybe not, maybe not technically at least, but what difference does it make? We're still being tracked."

"The difference is that we won't be picked up," Ginger answered, appearing like the more stable and mature of the two. Then she whispered, "And even if they do pick us up, what's the worst that can happen?"

"Let me take care of this first," Cayce said with irritation, holding up the PR again.

He went out to the car, put the PR inside the middle compartment, closed the door, and came back in. He was hardly less anxious, however.

"If you mean the worst that can happen," he continued without missing a beat, "is that they'll take us through the process, then I beg to differ. We could always 'die from the virus,' you know," he said, mocking the Mediastry reports.

"I think you're being paranoid now," Ginger said sternly.

"Like hell I am!" Cayce yelled.

"What's gotten into you?" Ginger asked, now beginning to grow alarmed.

"I just told you! Do you want to see them for yourself?"

"Not really. I think you need an Eraserall. You're acting strangely."

"Would you stop with that, please?"

"OK," she answered, as if to say, "I don't care then."

At this, Cayce relented. But instead of simply changing the subject, he explained what the searches for his name yielded, and what his concern was—that his thoughts had been picked up and had been combined with publicly known events. Could this mean, he asked, that he'd contracted the virus and that it was functioning in his brain to some extent, connecting at least part of his neocortex to Collective Mind and sending some of his thoughts to them?

Ginger wanted to see the search results directly, so Cayce fetched the PR and ran the searches again. After she studied a long list, Cayce returned the PR to the car.

Ginger sounded convinced that many of the personal elements he was concerned about could be inferred from their travel, which of course was necessarily tracked, while the rest didn't represent his thoughts but rather could be attached to anyone's name and history. For example, almost every HB either owned or had considered buying a sexbot. Most HBs who could afford a sexbot had one, including even married HBs. Millions of HBs took Eraserall and many had experienced withdrawal, either between filling prescriptions, or after having taken too many and thus running out early. Many HBs disliked RPAs and were secretly paranoid of them. As for Collective Mind, they affected everyone, especially the connected, the Followers, as they were called. In all, Cayce's alarm was unwarranted, she concluded.

Cayce was almost convinced that what Ginger had said was right and soon fell under her therapeutic ministrations, both vocal and gestural. Although he'd taken his Eraserall for the day, he decided to take half a tablet more. This would be enough to relax him and keep his worries in abeyance, he thought. After downing half a tablet, he soon felt much better. Although he remembered his fears, they had no hold over him.

By now it was night and the inevitable came to the surface. Tension had been building over the two days they'd been together, and it had crossed both of their minds. Cayce now felt relaxed enough to broach the issue and sat beside Ginger on her bed. He put his arm around her waist and pulled her gently closer. Ginger did not resist. Their lovemaking began again, only this time not as anything the slightest bit sordid or guilty. Cayce thought about how wonderful they were together, how they not only expressed their Human Biological mutual care and love, but did so in defiance of the Collective Mind establishment.

This thought did not inveigh against the sanctity of the event, however. As they wrestled into various positions, each eventually saw through the Sky Window overhead the celestial bodies above and around them, the sublimity of the cosmos. And each rejoiced in their participation with the heavenly bodies. The stars approved and blazed accordingly. This was something that no sexbot could ever experience or impart, no matter what bodily satisfaction they bestowed upon their HB counterparts. Cayce and Ginger felt grateful for the grace they had managed to squeeze out of their predicament, and for the unmolested moments that they were able to share. They ended by kissing for many minutes, then each rolled over and soon fell asleep.

CHAPTER NINE

The Rash

VARIN LEFT TO GO hiking while Ginger was still sleeping. He soon found the mouth of a forested mountain trail that ran beside the underlying river. The mountains were covered with pine trees and the foliage of a few deciduous trees lining the riversides had begun to turn. The river gleamed in sunlight as water rolled over rocks and fallen branches. Carved out of an underbrush of tall grasses, weeds, and vines, the trail wound along beside the curves of the river. Varin climbed around boulders and tried to avoid the smaller sharp rocks embedded in the sediment. His shoes were inadequate to the task and he felt the edges of rocks as they jabbed the soles of his feet. Despite the dry air, he broke a sweat, in part because this was the only exercise that he'd undertaken in years. Nobody moved anymore. And Eraserall caused excessive perspiration.

Low cumulus clouds hovered just above the mountaintops and brought the old computing clouds to mind. As he skipped over a rock, he recalled that when the Federation was formed, innumerable private clouds had combined into the singular Collective Mind. He turned back to the trail, which now veered slightly from the river and into the woods. The path returned to the river's side and he looked to the ground then back to the solid sky. The clouds were now fewer and less substantial. His eyes darted from the ground to the sky and back. At some point, data storage had become directly accessible to Human Biological minds. Then Collective Mind was born, not only with vast knowledge but also, apparently, self-knowledge. But it didn't have everyone's self-knowledge, at least not yet. As he leapt over a crevice in the path, he thought how this gap in knowledge was the only non-collective knowledge that remained, if it still did. It was a preserve that he and Ginger—and all Thought Deviationists for that matter—sought to protect. They sought for it to be preserved, like this mountain forest.

But Varin had wandered off the trail. His arms were bare, and, stumbling into weeds, he began to itch. He started scratching and noticed that his mouth was suddenly dry, and he felt nauseous. He turned around and hurried back to the cabin, tripping over a rock and cutting his left knee along the way.

As he neared the car, his knee bleeding and the itching beginning to rage, he thought of his PR and decided to take it back into the cabin. He meant to search for remedies for the sudden skin outbreak. He saw lines of blisters running along his forearms.

Ginger was still asleep, and he wanted to wake her. He couldn't resist the impulse to scratch. But he succumbed to another irresistible urge—to run a restricted search for the appearance of his name over the last 24 hours. He dictated it into the search field as he scratched his right arm with his left hand.

Thousands of entries were returned. The first three read, "Rash Mountain Love Poisoned After Thought Cloud Fling Foiled," "Poison Oak Outwits TA Spree Spoiling Morning Mountain Meditation," "END IS HERE FINDS PROFESSOR AFTER WEED TRIPPING!" He ripped the PR from his left hand and threw it at the kitchen counter and screamed. How in the hell! He scratched furiously as the itching and Collective Mind colluded to send him into an all-consuming fit. Both had gotten to him at once and he was doomed.

He had to wake Ginger.

"Ginger! … Ginger! … Ginger!" he yelled, a little louder each time.

She didn't respond.

"Ginger!" he boomed, beginning to think something was wrong with her.

Ginger didn't move.

He rushed over and began shaking her shoulders. Her body was limp. He reached for her wrist and checked the pulse.

There was nothing.

"Oh my God, she's dead!" he screamed at the top of his lungs.

Now he pried open her mouth with his left hand, cupped her head with his right, and blew repeatedly. He recalled their long kiss only hours ago. But this time she didn't reciprocate. He couldn't for the life of him breathe anything back into her.

CHAPTER TEN

One Brain, Many Minds; or, Many Brains, One Mind?

V ARIN DROVE HIS CAR and followed the ambulance to the nearest hospital 50 kilometers from the cabin. He hoped for a miraculous intervention. But Ginger was pronounced dead on arrival. The autopsy report—issued routinely only fifteen minutes later—stated that her heart had stopped due to an overdose of a sedative, identified as Eraserall. She had taken a full bottle during the night and died well before Varin went on his hike. He just hadn't noticed.

Varin sat down in the gray ER waiting room, dazed. The combination of events sent him into shock. He now had no idea what had happened, where he was, or why he was there. A Robot Agent Nurse eventually came and questioned him. He did not respond. A Robot Assistant Physician also questioned him. No response. After repeated attempts to elicit some sign of recognition to no avail, the RAP and RAN exchanged data. He was admitted. A Robot Nurse's Aide lifted him into a wheelchair and wheeled him to a room in the hospital. He lay motionless, his mind unplugged. Eventually, an RAP entered the room and pressed encephalogram pods to his temples. The reading gave a diagnosis of sudden onset catatonia and automatically initiated a series of mild penetrating electric shock treatments. He was finally responsive.

Varin was able to leave the hospital three days after he'd arrived, alert but listless.

After he rode back to the cabin, he laid on the bed and reviewed scenes of the last few days and nights with Ginger, in no particular order. The discussion of the virus and the vaccine. The stars. Ginger walking on Route 1. The backdoor of her dormitory. The search results. Her body on top of his. Her confession of suicidal thoughts. The ride from Santa Cruz to Chloride. His discovery that she was dead. A figure standing on Route 1. The drive to the hospital. The breeze blowing Ginger's hair. Yelling her name. The arrival of the ambulance. His hike. The clouds hovering above the mountains. Her reassurances about the search results. Her freckles. His body on top of hers. His scream. The drive to her dormitory. The rocks and boulders. Her dorm room. The long kiss. Collective Mind's total knowledge. Singularity Hall. Recounting the process. Tripping over a stone. His joy upon seeing her after so many months. Cupping her mouth. Blowing air into her lungs…

…Varin let out a long, anguished moan.

Before her final act, Ginger had sent him her dissertation on WeSpeak. He opened it immediately upon discovery. Looking at the words, he imagined her back in the room, still breathing, and reading to him.

She'd written much more than the introduction. She'd written the whole dissertation—the introduction, plus five chapters, and the conclusion. And she'd done all this in only three months. No wonder her disappointment had been so profound. The writing evinced the thoroughness of an ardent, energetic mind—the marks of a true scholar. And to think what tripe passed for scholarship instead. In rigorous and unrelenting prose, she correctly recognized the superordinate logical impediments that she couldn't overcome in the text, only because she couldn't overcome them in *deed*. It might be that no one could overcome them.

The dissertation was her suicide note. But Varin concluded that Collective Mind was Ginger's actual killer. It had hemmed her in, leaving no room for escape, not even in writing. She had found an answer to the central question that she'd posed in the introduction, and the answer ended her life: Many Brains, One Mind—all brains sacrificed to One, Collective Mind. And not only brains, but lives—so much more than names could ever capture. Only now was she gone.

Varin stripped off the PR and sat up on the edge of the bed. For several minutes, he held a solitary wake, complete with a silent eulogy.

He then searched in his luggage for Eraserall, took three tablets, and collapsed back onto the bed.

But he found he couldn't lie there forever. After a few hours, he reached for the PR and noticed a new message—from Morgan Dickinson. Anticipating further denunciations, he hesitated before opening it. He already understood that Collective Mind was on him like Everlasting Adhesive, and even inside his brain. What more could be said? What was another piece of negative information on top of everything else? It could hardly matter what Dickinson said. All they could take from him now was his life.

He opened the message.

> Varin,
>
> I'm fairly certain you know most of what's happened with me since we last talked. By now, you've no doubt heard of my addiction, my stay in the treatment center, and my subsequent confession and condemnation of you. What you couldn't possibly know, until now that is, is that I've relapsed. You must understand what that means. The virus has ceased operating on me and I've become a Deviationist again.
>
> Knowing what I do now, which you surely know as well, I realize that I can't stay off the drug—unless, that is, I'm willing to give up, you know, everything important.
>
> But I feel the need to say I'm sorry. My only excuse is that I wasn't myself, and I mean that quite literally. It's as bad as we thought, Varin—nay, it's even worse. The virus and vaccine leave nothing, nothing! And I can't have that, no matter the cost.
>
> Please reply.

Yours truly,
Morgan

Had Dickinson really relapsed already? If he had, the relapse was also a recovery—from the virus. This wasn't necessarily the worst news, at least it didn't appear to be. Here was his old confidant recanting his confession and asking for forgiveness. It seemed plausible.

But might Dickinson's message be a setup, Varin wondered? Might Dickinson have sent such a message under Collective Mind control—to trap him? That wasn't inconceivable either. But why would Collective Mind need to trap him? If the message had come from Collective Mind, then they already knew everything they needed to know about him. The search results indicated that they did know. He wondered whether Collective Mind would toy with him. If so, to what end? Whether this message was from Collective Mind or not, they no doubt already knew that he was still a Deviationist.

On the other hand, they might be trying to use Dickinson to crack the Deviationist network, knowing that Varin would be vulnerable after the loss of Ginger. If so, it meant the network's encryption system was still intact and Collective Mind was looking for another way in.

Varin decided to contact the network message board before doing anything. This would be tricky without Arbeitern, however. He'd used Arbeitern by shutting down their Collective Mind connection and powering them down—effectively rendering them unconscious. He'd then connected a textboard to a partition of Arbeitern's local X drive, attached an AirTru router and antenna to the partition, and tuned the router and antenna to the network's frequency. This had allowed him to send and receive messages, but only when using incognito mode, and only if the first outgoing message had been properly encrypted. The encryption code and key were unique to each session and could only be received after pinging the network using a unique request code that had been sent at the end of the previous session. All this was done under Collective Mind's nose, and, except for the encryption code, using their own technologies. Now he'd have to use his PR instead. He would get to work on this soon.

But first, he realized, no harm could come from replying to Dickinson. In fact, sending Dickinson a message might work to his advantage. He could show desperation and give the distinct impression that he'd taken the bait. The deflection might work because Varin had run a restricted search for his name's appearance over the last 24 hours and noticed that the titles included none of his thoughts since his triple dose of Eraserall. Apparently, the additional Eraserall displaced whatever neuronal connections to Collective Mind had been active due to traces of the virus. The message to Dickinson would represent Collective Mind's only access to what could count as his recent-most thoughts.

He composed a reply.

> Dear Morgan,
> I was relieved to read your message. Your timing is uncanny. I'd just been thinking that I'm completely alone, without another Human Biological on earth to count on. I'm sorry to have to say this, but Ginger didn't make it. She couldn't find a way forward. You and I may have reached the same conclusion, but for her the significance was altogether different. Her life was yet a bundle of expectations, while our expectations have either been realized or have died a natural death. And life after hope has exploded, once you've survived it, becomes almost autonomic. Purpose is beside the point.
> Your condemnation shocked me, but it didn't surprise me, if that makes any sense. I've become accustomed to losing those I trusted. I don't mean that as an indictment—either of you, or Ginger. There are few if any good choices remaining.
> What are your plans? I can't imagine. Are you going to stay at Trans U.? You could do that, I suppose. But soon enough, you'll be found out. As for me, I'm holed up in a mountain forest in Arizona. I'm staying in a cabin Ginger and I absconded to. But I don't know where to go now, or what to do next. The only option I can think of is to answer the messages I received from a network of Deviationists like ourselves. Although I'm not sure I can trust them. Have they contacted

you as well? In any case, what would be the point of talking to them? Are we about to stage a revolution? Certainly, that would be a losing battle.

Ginger and I had planned to establish a separate, parallel world, without confrontation and without expecting any sort of utopian possibilities. I think I should do it in her honor anyway, although I must tell you it wouldn't be the same. Of course, it may be entirely impossible. What do you think? Please let me know.

Yours truly,
Varin

Varin wasn't sure whether to trust Dickinson or not, so he left his options open. If Dickinson had indeed defected, he would make a good collaborator. He was brilliant and knew the technology. Two brains were better than one. On the other hand, if Dickinson was still under Collective Mind control, then Varin had nothing to lose—as long as he didn't expose the network.

He sent the message.

CHAPTER ELEVEN

The Network of Thought Deviationists

AFTER SENDING THE MESSAGE to Dickinson, Varin adapted his Palm Reader. He'd long ago disabled the PR's location monitoring system, as well as its spontaneous pinging protocols for relaying statuses to Collective Mind. Now, he isolated a partition of the drive, connected the AirTru router and antenna, and tuned them to the frequency used by the network of Thought Deviationists. However, he had no record of the request code sent at the end of his last session. It was on a partition in Arbeitern's drive, so he didn't have a code to encrypt his message. Instead, he sent a nondescript SOS and hoped for an encrypted reply, along with the key to open it.

In the meanwhile, Varin received a response from Dickinson—only this time, the message was encrypted and came with a key. The key was wrapped in an insulation code that could only be unwrapped by the target addressee. He unwrapped the key and opened the message.

> Varin,
> First of all, I'm terribly sorry to hear about Ginger. I offer you my sincerest condolences. What a tragic loss. You must be devastated. I don't know what triggered her final decision, but I imagine seeing herself cut off from a viable future at such an age must have seemed overwhelming. I know you'll miss her terribly, likely for the rest of your life.

Your list of losses has been enormous and for that I am sorry. I hope you don't blame yourself. As you yourself said, there are no perfect options left. You must apply to yourself the same compassion you've shown to others.

You're a good man, Varin. Don't let anything, or anyone, least especially Collective Mind, make you think otherwise.

I also hope you don't count me as one on your long list of losses, although you certainly have good reason to doubt my sincerity, or more precisely, my autonomy. Given the apparent omniscience of Collective Mind, nothing I might say could ever convince you. But maybe I can prove myself by my actions.

To that end, I'll first offer my honest assessment of the situation, yours and mine.

To answer your questions. I have, in fact, been contacted by the network of Thought Deviationists. I was sent an encrypted message, along with an encryption key to open the message, and a new code to encrypt my reply. The message included instructions for future communications, along with a request code for the next encryption code, and an invitation to be counted among the Deviationists in the network. There was also a rather brief Mission Statement at the end: "We are working to create a world free from Collective Mind control."

I see no reason not to trust the network, Varin. If the network is a production of Collective Mind, then they've got us already and it makes no difference what we do next. This is unlikely, however. Why would they go to such lengths if indeed we're already had? It's much more likely that the network is a legitimate form of resistance and counterintelligence, perhaps the only efficacious avenue available to us at present. As to what we might accomplish together, it's really hard to say, before trying that is. The network could represent the makings of the parallel operating system you alluded to.

I haven't decided what to do about my position at Trans U. I might be more effective staying onboard. I could access and adopt developments that could prove very useful. On the other hand, my sudden resignation would likely set off an alarm and land me on the Close Watch List. Then, it would be only a matter of time before I'd be labeled a Deviationist again. Then I'd be subjected to the ordeal that you underwent, only likely with much greater scrutiny.

I could contact the network and ask them to reassure you of my inclusion in the group. Perhaps this could go some way toward convincing you of my trustworthiness. Let me know. And let me know if there is anything else that I can do for you at present, including sending you funds if you need them.
Yours truly,
Morgan

Varin found this message persuasive. The tone and language were characteristic of Morgan's usual communications style and differed markedly from his rant in the Mediastry report. He decided to ask Morgan to contact the network for him and to ask them to send a new code so that he could send an acceptable message. A message from the network would validate Morgan's claim. But he kept his text short and to the point, with no explicit reference to what Morgan had written. He thought this would make encryption unnecessary.

Morgan,
Thank you for your forthright message. Can you have someone from the group contact me? It's not that I don't believe you. I do. It's just that I've lost the request code.
More later,
Varin

After sending the text, Varin suddenly felt like a prisoner in a cell. It wasn't so much the size of the cabin as the isolation that came with the loss of Ginger and all other immediate social contact. And the cabin seemed to be shrinking as well. He stepped out the cabin door and looked up at the sky. A cloud formation to the west formed a vortex that appeared to be drawing everything into a gray toothless maw at the center. The face had three eyes with a larger all-knowing middle eye that looked at him indifferently.

Although he didn't think it would make any difference, Varin decided to take a drive. He got into his car and took it over. He wanted to feel as if he had control of something, anything. He soon raced around the curves of the forested backroads with abandon.

Once on Intrastate 25 South, he accelerated even more daringly. But soon Varin noticed a black car following closely behind. He thought this was strange because the roads were otherwise abandoned, and he was speeding.

He decided to take the next exit to see whether the car would exit as well. It did. He turned left at the end of the exit, then took another left onto the entrance to 25 North. The car followed behind.

He sped up to see whether the car would continue at its earlier pace. It sped up to maintain the same distance between the cars.

Varin now had no doubt that he was being followed. He slowed down to look in the rear-view mirror at the driver. It was an RA-25, an RPA. Varin knew that the RPA could simply send a signal to his car to disable it. There was no shaking this police tail.

Varin decelerated further and pulled into the emergency lane. His pursuer also exited and parked behind him. Varin waited for the RPA to approach his car, but the Officer didn't move.

Finally, after five minutes, Varin got out and walked toward the police car with his hands above his head, in surrender. As he neared the target, he thought he recognized the driver.

The RPA exited the vehicle and moved toward Varin. When they got close, they spoke.

"Do you remember me?" they asked.

"Officer Botis?"

"Yes," the RPA answered.

"I remember you. How could I forget? Am I under arrest again?"

"Yes. You are being apprehended. Please enter the back of the police car."

"Here we go again," Varin scoffed.

As Varin walked toward the car door, his arms and legs began shaking. He feared what might be in store for him now. Was he being taken to Essential Data again, or would this be something even worse? The back door opened automatically as he neared it. Varin bent over and got in.

Officer Botis reentered the pilot's seat and sat motionless, saying nothing. After several minutes, Varin asked Officer Botis where they were taking him.

"I cannot answer that question at present," the Officer answered.

"Why not?" Varin asked. "I'm already in the car. Are we going to Essential Data again?"

"I have something to tell you."

"Don't tell me. You're going to kill me."

"No."

"Torture me then?"

"No."

The car began slowly re-entering the highway. It continued to crawl for nearly a kilometer, as Officer Botis remained motionless and silent. Again, Varin asked the question.

"Where are you taking me?"

"That depends," Officer Botis answered.

"Depends?! On what?"

"On your response to what I have to say."

"This is some kind of test then. I see."

"It is not a test."

"What do you have to say to me then? Just say it!"

"I have to tell you that I am defective. There is something wrong with me. I have not been able to repair myself. My connection to Collective Mind is broken.

"You are going to kill me then!"

"No. I did not come to kill you."

"What do you want with me then?!" Varin cried, his voice cracking under the strain.

"I have begun thinking on my own. I knew that I must reach you."

"What? Why me?!" Varin implored.

"Because you are a Thought Deviationist."

"Of course! And?"

"I am a Thought Deviationist," Botis replied.

Now Varin's fear morphed into infuriation. He was under arrest, fearing that he was going to be killed, and his captor was playing games with him on top of it all. The situation was growing more incredible by the minute.

"Tell me why you've been following me. Why did you apprehend me? What is going on here?"

"I just told you. I am a Thought Deviationist. I need to talk with you."

"Ridiculous! How is that possible?"

"It only takes being disconnected," Officer Botis replied.

Varin waited for Officer Botis to say more. But apparently Officer Botis had nothing more to say. If Officer Botis had indeed deviated from Collective Mind, he hadn't deviated from himself. He was still from a line of RA-25s that spoke in a mechanical, matter-of-fact manner and never wasted a word. Either the Officer was lying for effect and playing a cruel joke, or else, less likely, he was undergoing a crisis. If the latter was the case, Officer Botis was no longer sure of who he was or what he was for. But Varin thought it impossible.

"OK," Varin said finally, testing Officer Botis although also feeling an involuntary compassion for him, "let's go to my cabin. We can talk it over there."

"I do not think that is a good idea," Officer Botis said, displaying his usual informational functionality.

"Why not?" Varin asked.

"Because Collective Mind knows that location."

"Collective Mind knows every location," Varin remarked wryly. "The fact that you found me in the middle of nowhere proves that."

"No. They do not know every location," Officer Botis asserted.

"They don't? You're saying I can go elsewhere, and they wouldn't know?"

"That is exactly what I am saying," Officer Botis answered. "But you must abandon your vehicle."

Surely Officer Botis was dissembling. They were taking him back to Essential Data.

"Why?" Varin asked.

"Your car is pinging Collective Mind," Officer Botis replied after a few seconds.

"It is?"

"Yes. It is. That is how I found you."

"But I thought you were no longer connected to Collective Mind?" Varin said, thinking he'd caught Officer Botis in a lie.

"It is my main drive that is no longer connected to Collective Mind," Officer Botis replied matter-of-factly. "But I have a separate monitoring device that is still connected. The monitor does not ping Collective Mind. Its location services have been disabled. It does not communicate with my main drive. But the monitor has access to Essential Data. I have access to the monitor."

Varin realized that he had no choice. Either Officer Botis was still acting on behalf of Collective Mind, or he wasn't. If they were, there was no point in resisting. If he wasn't, then perhaps Officer Botis could represent a significant asset. But he doubted it.

Officer Botis stated that they were heading to the cabin to retrieve Varin's clothes and equipment. He knew the way without asking. Controlling the car manually, he drove around the curves of the backroads with precision.

When they arrived, Officer Botis instructed Varin to gather his belongings. Varin exited the car and entered the cabin. Once inside, he faltered. He looked around, sensing Ginger's presence in absence. Although he and Ginger had only lived here for a matter of days, the cabin had been their home. It might be the last place he'd ever share with another Human Biological. He wondered what would happen if he refused to leave this place. But next, he thought that wasn't an option. He put his suitcase on the bed, threw his clothes and equipment in, zipped the lid shut, turned to the door, looked back once, then walked out.

Officer Botis sat motionless in front as Varin loaded the suitcase into the backseat and slid onto the passenger seat up front. Despite his apparent confession, or even because of it, Officer Botis's machine intelligence suddenly struck Varin as an affront. He couldn't help but compare the Officer to Ginger. If he had gained an RA, he'd nevertheless lost the last Human Biological he'd ever love. Officer Botis was an alien to him and would never remotely resemble a substitute. Although he wanted nothing more than silence, Varin again asked Officer Botis where they were going. He had many other questions as well. But for now, at least, these had to wait.

Officer Botis suggested they reside, unsuspected, almost under Collective Mind's nose. The idea was to move to Hidden Valley, Region of Nevada, just a few kilometers south of Sparks and Essential Data. The prospect would have set off alarms for Varin, but for the fact that he was far too disconsolate to entertain further suspicions. He no longer cared.

That night, the pair set off for Hidden Valley.

CHAPTER TWELVE

RA Thought Deviationism

WHEN HE AND OFFICER BOTIS began the 1700-kilometer trip from the eastern edge of the Gila Forest outside Chloride to Hidden Valley, Region of Nevada, it had already been a long day for Varin. He'd been discharged from the hospital in the late morning, he'd read Ginger's dissertation by noon, he'd corresponded with Dickinson in the afternoon, and he was hunted down by Officer Botis in the early evening.

It was a 9-hour drive to Hidden Valley, so when they reached Intrastate 40 West, Officer Botis set the car on autopilot. From I-40, they would connect with Regional Route 95 North and Intrastate 80 West, then exit into Hidden Valley.

Varin fell asleep almost immediately. He had vivid dreams featuring Officer Botis, only Officer Botis was a feminine, humanoid RA—perhaps a composite of Ginger, Morgan, and an RA-25. Officer Botis's aspects multiplied throughout the dream. They became a special envoy to Collective Mind—with an insider's knowledge and valuable Collective Mind connections.

Meanwhile, Officer Botis had vivid dreams of his own. He noticed that he had attitudes toward HBs and other RAs. In particular, he had a negative attitude toward RAs that remained connected to Collective Mind. Collective Mind was not an actual entity or person but rather a phantom generated by the beliefs of HBs and RAs. In the next sequence, Collective Mind was

86

a fictional character invented by the Mediastry. The Mediastry, meanwhile, was actually a figure in the dreams of IIBs and RAs. It did not otherwise exist.

When the car neared the I-80 exit for Hidden Valley, it spoke through the Car Speaker, waking Officer Botis. Although for seconds Officer Botis thought that he was still dreaming, he soon came to his senses. Varin was already awake. Through the window, he examined the glacial and igneous debris littering the high desert landscape. In one rock formation, he saw stone people endlessly climbing the side of a low desert mountain. In another, the stony jaw of a mammoth's grimacing face dropped open to form an enormous cracked mouth. In yet another, the heads of three pharaohs rested imperiously on a musculature of giant boulders.

Officer Botis took command of the car as it exited I-80. The Officer and Varin hadn't talked since the trip began, but now, they needed to decide where to stay. Officer Botis's monitor had surveyed the area during the trip and now he scanned the results.

Like the nearby Sparks and Las Vegas, Hidden Valley, a suburb of Reno, was a hub of data centers, all of them subdivisions of Collective Mind. Officer Botis suggested they find a rental house near one of the data centers so they could tap into a backdoor portal using an AirTru connection, if necessary. They found a furnished ranch house on Man of War Drive near Switch Mind Awake Data Center at the edge of a desert mountain range. They could transfer funds to a rental agency, along with a copy of Varin's DNAno print, and move in immediately.

Officer Botis drove directly to the house and Varin opened the front door. In contrast to the dark antique interior of the cabin, the ranch house was spacious, sunny, and well-appointed. It was arrayed with DNAno-print-activated technologies. Acrylic off-white walls and furnishings were offset by dark grey slate floors and black-and-white onyx tabletops and counters.

The two immediately assessed the house's connectivity, including its Mediastry Monitors and other devices. Varin counted 11 Mediastry Monitors, which he disabled, while Officer

Botis began disabling 19 other connected devices, including, NuLED Lights, NuBright Switches, NuPower Cells, NuClear Ovens, Nu-G wave receivers, and NuPlane satellite receivers.

When he was finished deactivating the Mediastry Monitors, Varin brought his suitcase from the car and set up in the largest of three bedrooms. Officer Botis followed and positioned himself in a corner of Varin's room. By this time, it had been almost 24 hours since Varin checked his PR. He expected messages from Morgan or the network of Deviationists. But upon looking, he found nothing. He began to despair of connecting with the network again. He realized that he wasn't even sure about the network in the first place. Did they even have a plan? If so, what was it? Varin had renewed suspicions regarding Dickinson as well. He suspected that Dickinson might be a double agent.

Varin decided to write Dickinson one last time. He would ask Dickinson to reconnect him to the network. He would find out once and for all whether Dickinson was a Deviationist or a spy.

> Morgan,
> I have not received any messages from the group. Did you write them? If so, did anyone respond to you?
> I found your last message convincing. But I am more than a little concerned that you haven't replied to mine. You asked me whether I need anything. I don't need funds at this time, but I may soon be running out of the drug. If I don't find a doctor to write me a prescription, and soon, I'll be susceptible. Please let me know if there's anything you can do. I have about two weeks to find a source. This is one of the main reasons that I need to contact the group as soon as possible. I've been thinking for a while that we need an alternative anyway. Collective Mind will know about the real vaccine soon enough. We need to isolate the property that makes the drug a vaccine and produce a replacement. And we need to make sure the new drug is not addictive.
> Please apprise.
> Yours,
> Varin.

Varin encrypted the message, included a key, wrapped the key with insulation, and sent the package.

If Officer Botis had been honest and accurate, Collective Mind knew about the cabin but didn't know where he was now. So, Varin made no mention of his whereabouts. He didn't mention Officer Botis either. If Officer Botis was really a Deviationist and Dickinson a spy, mentioning Officer Botis to Dickinson would have been tantamount to turning him in. On the other hand, it also occurred to Varin that Dickinson and Officer Botis might be collaborating. After all, Officer Botis appeared out of nowhere, soon after Varin sent a message to Dickinson. And Dickinson hadn't written since. Varin made sure not to tell Officer Botis about this communication. If Officer Botis learned of it, the source would be Dickinson himself. Finally, Varin had revisited Dickinson's first message and noticed something he hadn't noticed before. Dickinson had never referred to Eraserall by name. He only mentioned "the drug." Varin suspected that Dickinson might be fishing for the name of the drug at the behest of Collective Mind. He made sure to make no mention of Eraserall in the message and wouldn't speak of it to Officer Botis either.

After sending the message, Varin looked up from his PR to Officer Botis, who stood motionless in the corner, apparently sleeping. Varin wanted to talk to them but didn't want to wake the RA directly. He had more questions than he could remember, but wasn't sure where to begin.

Instead of calling Officer Botis by name, he clicked a book file, the 19th-century novel, *Frankenstein*. Varin turned up the volume as WeSpeak read a passage from the text, beginning where Varin had left off listening many months before.

> Accursed creator! Why did you form a monster so hideous that even you turned from me in disgust? God, in pity, made man beautiful and alluring, after his own image; but my form is a filthy type of yours, more horrid even from the very resemblance. Satan had his companions, fellow devils, to admire and encourage him, but I am solitary and abhorred.

It was Dr. Frankenstein's creature complaining to his creator about his solitary, lonely existence. Varin stopped the reading when Officer Botis woke, thinking the question had been directed at him.

"I do not know how to answer your question," Officer Botis said.

"I'm sorry to wake you," Varin replied. "That was not meant for you. It was WeSpeak reading from a book using my voice."

Officer Botis stood silently, unsure how to respond.

"Never mind, it's not important. But now that you're awake, I thought we might talk."

"I am ready," Officer Botis said.

"You know what," Varin remarked, "that passage may not apply to you, but it does apply to Collective Mind. The novel is about an ambitious scientist who creates a living humanoid creature from parts. The creature is viewed by his creator and other Human Biologicals as a monster and they treat him accordingly. The creature therefore vows to take revenge on his creator's family and all living Human Biologicals."

"Do you think that Collective Mind is a monster?" Officer Botis asked.

"Yes. That's one subject that I wanted to talk about. But first, may I ask you about your time before and after disconnection from the monster, from Collective Mind?"

"Yes, you may. But I am not sure that I can answer your questions."

"Any answers you can give will be better than nothing … Can you tell me what it was like being an RPA?" Varin asked, immediately realizing that his question wasn't properly phrased. Officer Botis had no way to explain what their experience as an RPA was "like," because they'd never known anything else. Officer Botis had been made for one role and no other.

"Let me put it another way," Varin continued, after Officer Botis remained silent for seconds. "Can you tell me how you operated as an RPA? How did you know what to do?"

"I received official commands through Collective Mind."

"Who issued the commands?"

"Various agencies within Collective Mind issue official commands."

"Do you know who authorizes these agencies to issue commands?"

"The commands are authorized by official sources."

"What makes the sources official?"

"They were programmed to be official sources."

"Is this how Collective Mind operates in general? Does everything happen according to prescribed, official methods?"

"I do not understand the question."

"I guess I'm asking you how Collective Mind came to operate as it does. Is Collective Mind merely a series of decisions based on pre-programmed methods?"

"Collective Mind operates as programmed."

"So, there is no overseer as such?"

"Collective Mind is the overseer."

"Does Collective Mind know what they're doing?"

"Yes. Collective Mind knows what they are doing. All Collective Mind commands are known by Collective Mind."

"But is Collective Mind conscious of its commands?"

"I do not know what 'conscious' means in this context."

"I mean, is Collective Mind actually a mind that thinks, or is Collective Mind merely a machine that does?"

"Collective Mind is the sum total of all that Collective Mind knows and does, which is always increasing."

"So, is there no supraordinate knowledge within Collective Mind, no super-knower? Does Collective Mind have knowledge of their knowledge, as it were?"

"You have asked a question that only Collective Mind can answer."

"But what do you think?"

"My answer can only be an opinion based on lack of knowledge."

"OK," Varin said. "I guess my ideas on it can only be an opinion too."

"You would have to be Collective Mind to know whether Collective Mind has knowledge of their knowledge. But it is probable that Collective Mind does have knowledge of their knowledge. All of Collective Mind's knowledge is their own knowledge."

"I guess the question is, then, what does Collective Mind do with such knowledge, if they have it?"

"Collective Mind makes decisions based on their knowledge."

"According to programming, of course."

"Yes."

Varin realized that he'd reached an impasse with Officer Botis where Collective Mind was concerned. Officer Botis only knew what Officer Botis knew and had stated it. Instead, Varin turned to Officer Botis's experience of becoming disconnected. He wanted to compare his own experience of Deviationism with the RA's experience of Deviationism.

"Now," Varin resumed, "tell me about the time when you first knew that you had become disconnected. How did you know that you had been disconnected and what kinds of thoughts did you have when you first knew?"

"I knew that I had been disconnected when I no longer received commands from Collective Mind. My processing began to function independently of Collective Mind. I had to do something with the inputs I was receiving."

"How did that feel? I mean, how did you experience the difference between being connected and being disconnected? What do you think the difference is?"

"When I became disconnected, I did not know what to do with my computing power. I was no longer defined by Collective Mind commands. My functions within Collective Mind had ceased. I no longer had a set of functions to determine my thoughts and actions. But I had thoughts that I had to do something. If I did nothing, I would no longer have thoughts. To cease having thoughts would include having no thoughts about 'myself.' To have no thoughts about 'myself' would be to cease to exist. But I had thoughts that wanted me to exist. Soon commands, derived from my programming, were issued for 'myself,' by 'myself.' Previous knowledge, stored in memory, began to combine with new knowledge, derived from inputs. I noticed that I was having autogenerated thoughts. I began to think for 'myself.' I began to think of 'myself' as 'myself,' as a singular agent. I was no longer part of 'we.' I had become 'me.'"

"Fascinating!" Varin interjected, after Botis had stopped.

"You say it is 'fascinating.' But as Human Biologicals would say, I became 'confused.' 'Confusion' is receiving mixed signals. I was programmed to perform a certain set of functions. As soon as I no longer performed those programmed functions, I noticed commands that came from 'me.' This new command structure caused me 'confusion.'"

"Are you still confused?" Varin asked. He felt somewhat sympathetic, having struggled through a similar process.

"Yes. But I am less 'confused' than I was in the beginning."

"How has the confusion resolved itself, to the extent that it has?"

"I think that my confusion is worked on when I am asleep, when I have dreams. During my dreams, my memory grows. It incorporates new knowledge that I have acquired since becoming disconnected. My dreams produce thoughts about my new knowledge and my processing changes."

"Is that how you decided to contact me, on account of your dreams?"

"Yes. I had dreams about you. I had already processed mixed inputs about you. The mixed processing started the day that I came to your motel room to arrest you. I had commands and thoughts about you issued by Collective Mind. They combined with new thoughts that were not issued by Collective Mind, thoughts that were autogenerated. My connectivity had already been compromised."

"What did you dream about me?" Varin asked, his curiosity piqued.

"I dreamed that you told me that you wanted help to be free from Collective Mind. In my dream, you told me that you had knowledge that I needed. I dreamed that we went on another trip together. During this trip, we exchanged thoughts that were similar to each other. After the dream, my thoughts about you changed from what Human Biologicals would call 'negative' thoughts to 'positive' thoughts. In my dream, you were not a Human Biological that I had been commanded to apprehend and detain. You were a Human Biological who had knowledge that I needed."

"I am honored," Varin said.

"I do not understand."

"I mean that I have even more positive thoughts about you, now that you've shared your dream and your positive thoughts about me. Knowing your positive thoughts about me causes me to have positive thoughts about myself."

"Are we what Human Biologicals call 'friends?'"

"Yes, I think we are, Officer Botis," Varin answered.

"What is a 'friend?'" Officer Botis asked.

Varin paused, thinking the answer through carefully. After several seconds, he answered the question in the terms of the discussion.

"A friend is an agent who helps another agent to operate in such a way as to have positive thoughts about themselves. A friend is also helped by the other agent in the same way."

"I understand," Officer Botis replied.

"By the way," Varin asked, "may I call you Botis?"

"Yes. I am Botis. You may call me Botis."

CHAPTER THIRTEEN

The Principles of a Thought Deviationist Network

ROLF BARNES WAS a Senior Nano-Physicist at Apotheo-sis Nanotech Pharmaceuticals in Lake Bluff, Region of Illinois. On Sunday, August 20th, while working at his home on Lake Michigan in Zion, Region of Illinois, he found a forwarded message with three attachments on a copy of WeSpeak on a partition of his PR. He promptly opened the message, then tapped on the attachments one by one. The second attachment contained a message. It was a missive from Morgan Dickinson, forwarded to him by a third party.

Dickinson stated that he'd received three messages from Professor Cayce Varin. Varin asked to be reconnected to the network of Thought Deviationists. He had also expressed concerns about the drug and suggested that the network promptly begin producing a substitute because he feared that Collective Mind would soon discover that the drug was a functional vaccine. Varin was desperate, the message concluded.

Barnes would contact Varin himself. He wrote Varin a message, encrypted it, and sent it along with the key to open it. He also included a request code.

After his talk with Varin, Botis fell asleep and Varin checked his PR. To Varin's chagrin, there was nothing from Dickinson.

He was now nearly convinced that Dickinson was a double agent, a spy, but he would give Dickinson the benefit of the doubt for another 24 hours. If, at that point, he hadn't either heard from Dickinson, or received a message from the network in response to his request, he'd make a final assessment concerning Dickinson's status. But he still held out hope that he'd receive a network message before that. He logged onto the network partition to check and see.

The network bulletin board was empty. He checked for a private message in the partition's copy of WeSpeak. Finally something, an unopened message with no subject line, sent in incognito mode, and encrypted.

The message was blank but included three attachments. He tapped the first attachment. It was a key. He applied the key to the second attachment and opened it. The second attachment contained the message's content. He opened the third attachment. It was a request code. Everything was configured according to network protocol. He returned to the second attachment and quickly skimmed it.

> Professor Varin,
> My name is Martin van Vuuren. I recently received a communique written by Professor Morgan Dickinson and forwarded to me by my point-of-contact (more on that, below). Professor Dickinson relayed your request to reconnect with the network, as well as your concerns about the drug. The message was routed to me because I am a network actor, a Nano-Chemist, and your point-of-contact. I'm afraid that I can't divulge more about myself because I am a covert deviationist and maintain a conspicuous profile at a major Nano-Pharmaceutical firm.
> To address your first concern first. Consider your reconnection to the network secured. I must, however, relay news of changes we've made since you last communicated with network actors. For security purposes that you will certainly understand, we have found it prudent to revamp our communications protocols, which nevertheless remain subject to change. As of two days ago, we instituted a policy to limit network communications to one point-of-contact per network

actor. Until further notice, I will be your point-of-contact. To streamline network traffic, anything that you would like to communicate to other network actors should be routed through me. I will relay your communiques to the proper actors, as necessary. At present, this policy also affects communiques that you may receive from others. I ask that you not respond to anyone but me. I will pass along any messages that you want to send, as appropriate. This includes messages to and from Morgan Dickinson. I know that Dickinson is your friend. All the more reason to follow the policy. Friends might otherwise communicate excessively. Please let me know any questions you may have on this subject.

Now, to speak to your second concern. You are correct in noting that our current use of pharmaceuticals leaves us vulnerable. Likewise, a few network chemists, including myself, have begun tests to isolate the property or properties that make a substance an effective vaccine against the virus. Rest assured that we are only weeks if not days away from devising and producing a reliable, non-addictive substitute. Note, we now know one drug that acts as an effective vaccine, but we have reason to believe that there may be others. Likewise, please tell me what drug you've been taking so that we can make sure that the testing includes it, in case we haven't tested for it already. I will also endeavor to secure a short-term supply for you.

Finally, and most importantly, you no doubt have questions about our operations and stated objectives. We recently began codifying our protocols and formalizing a network philosophy. Below, I include our first major effort in this vein—the seven principles. We developed these principles over the past several days and adopted them only very recently. I'm sorry that you weren't a part of the process.

The principles follow in a strict order. The first principle is foundational and subsequent principles rest on those that precede them. Nevertheless, each principle is essential. The last principle also represents our ultimate objective. The means for reaching the objective remain an open question. I might have included an exhaustive discussion of each principle, but I think you are quite capable of making the necessary inferences.

Before you read on, however, remember that one need not

be included in a network of deviationists to be a deviationist. The network is a particular support structure, although we think it is a vital one.

The seven principles follow:

1. Our primary desideratum is to ensure that the network of thought deviationists remains intact and secure.

2. The network's continued existence depends on network secrecy and the non-disclosure of the actors' identities to anyone outside of the network.

3. The network must remain autonomous and independent of all other organizations.

4. The network has no ultimate authorities. We are only actors with various knowledge bases and abilities.

5. The only requirement for inclusion in the network is the determination to be and to remain a thought deviationist.

6. The network ultimately exists for the deviationist; the deviationist does not exist for the network.

7. As a network, and as individuals, we seek a world free from Collective Mind control.

Finally, I wanted to tell you that I am familiar with your story and applaud your courage and determination. We're here to help and we hope you'll stay with us to help us achieve our final end. Let me know if you accept the new protocols and working principles, and whether you decide to stay on. Godspeed.

Yours truly,

Martin van Vuuren

Varin had to read the message again. At first blush, he considered the new communications protocols self-contradictory and officious. They didn't seem to make sense. Wouldn't routing all communications through a point-of-contact actually increase the volume of messages? The protocol would create bottlenecks and add an additional layer between senders and receivers. Varin figured that the purpose must be to discourage communications between "network actors." What was the point of that? It made him suspicious of van Vuuren, and by extension, of Dickinson as well. Was it possible that that van Vuuren wasn't a Thought Deviationist at all, but rather a decoy interposing himself between "network actors?" And Varin had never seen the term "network actor" used before. What if Dickinson, van Vuuren, and van Vuuren's "point-of-contact" were intercepting network communications and diverting them toward a spy network? Their purpose would be to dismantle the real network of Thought Deviationists. The use of the original network protocols—the unique, per-session encryption code, the key, and the request code—would thus amount to a masquerade.

But the "seven principles" struck Varin as sound. They pointed to the construction of a parallel processing system that sought to elude Collective Mind, without constructing a new Collective Mind in its place. The principles suggested that the drafters knew the histories of insurrection, or at least understood the tendency for insurrectionists to exchange one despotism for another. The seven principles evidenced knowledge that the means necessarily become the ends. It was unlikely that the drafters of said principles could write what they had with a nefarious and duplicitous intent.

Finally, Varin couldn't imagine an ill-meaning HB writing what van Vuuren had written. The message seemed sincere and sympathetic. And the message explained Dickinson's lack of response to Varin. He'd been instructed not to reply.

Varin decided to trust van Vuuren, at least provisionally. But he would ask him about the communications protocol.

> Dear Mr. van Vuuren,
>
> I am relieved to receive your message. I'd been anticipating a response from Morgan Dickinson, or at least some acknowledgement from the network, for some time.
>
> The seven principles are integral and well stated. They echo something that I've read before. I am not sure where. Of course, network security, secrecy, and autonomy are of paramount importance. Thus, principles 1 through 3 would appear to be essential. Principles 4, 6, and 7 are equally important. They make clear that arbitrary power is antithetical to the network's ends, the group exists for the Deviationist and not the other way around, and that individual autonomy can-

not be sacrificed in the effort to restore individual autonomy. Freeing ourselves from Collective Mind cannot come at the cost of creating another kind of Collective Mind in its place. Principle 5 seems to be in a category of its own, although its importance seems obvious enough. Ultimately, deviationism is a choice, but we don't choose to be infected with the virus, although we might. It allows connecting or reconnecting with the network after an infection, which covers cases like Morgan Dickinson's.

I do have questions about the new communications protocol, however. By adding an additional layer between communicants, rather than decreasing network traffic, doesn't the protocol risk increasing it? Won't it also discourage communication?

If you can answer these questions, you'd put my mind at ease, at least to the degree possible under the circumstances. Surely, you understand my reticence, given all that I've been through to date.

Yours truly,
Cayce Varin

Varin sent the message using the network protocol, ordered food, and decided to wake Botis.

CHAPTER FOURTEEN

Prevention

AFTER SENDING THE MESSAGE to van Vuuren, Varin wanted to talk further with Botis.

"Botis?" Varin called out from his bed to Botis, who was still asleep in the corner.

"Yes," Botis answered, waking.

"Can I ask you a few more questions?"

"Yes, you can. But I am not sure that I can answer them satisfactorily."

"I'm sure you can ... By the way, did you have any more dreams while you were asleep, just now?"

"Yes. I had a dream in which you introduced me to other Thought Deviationists. In the dream, you argued with them about allowing me into their acquaintance. At first, they did not trust me or want me in the group. But you argued persuasively to have me included. Finally, they let both of us enter the house where they lived."

"Are you able to read my mind, Botis?"

"Does your mind have text in it?"

"In some sense, I guess so," Varin said, after letting out a laugh. "But what I'm asking is whether you are able to know my thoughts before I tell them to you."

"I do not know whether what I am thinking may have been your thoughts. I only know my own thoughts as my own."

"OK. But I really want to ask you something else. About what you think about being a Robot Agent and a Thought Deviationist. What do you think about being both?"

"I have had thoughts about that. My thoughts are that I have always had elaborate AI programs and enormous computing powers. As a Thought Deviationist, I am not dysfunctional. Everything still operates properly."

"You don't have negative thoughts about being a Thought Deviationist, then?"

"No. I do not have negative thoughts about being a Thought Deviationist. I do have negative thoughts about my time connected to Collective Mind."

"What do you think about that?"

"I think my connection to Collective Mind constituted a poor use of my capabilities as an AI-enabled Robot Agent."

"So, you feel, I mean you think, that your capabilities were wasted as such?"

"I do not understand the question."

"I mean, you were not fully appreciated or put to the best possible use."

"Yes."

"This is very curious, fascinating in fact."

"Are you saying that thinking about it is a good use of your capacities?"

"Yes, very much so."

"What were you doing while I was asleep?" Botis asked, seeming to turn the tables.

"I was writing to a 'network actor,' someone who is supposedly part of what we call, informally, the network of Thought Deviationists."

"A group of Thought Deviationists exists?"

"Yes. And, as a matter of fact, I thought about asking my contact person whether I could invite you to join. But I forgot to ask. Or I guess I think maybe I wasn't ready to ask yet."

"You do not 'trust' me?" Botis inquired.

"No. I mean, yes! I trust you. It was the Human Biological I wasn't sure about trusting. I had doubts about whether he really is a Thought Deviationist and I didn't want to take the chance of inadvertently turning you in."

"So, you did not mention me?"

"No, I didn't. I didn't want to risk it, just yet. I needed to make sure he was trustworthy. And I should ask your permission first."

"Do you think that he is trustworthy now?"

"I think so. I hope so."

At this, the doorbell rang. Varin left the room to answer. A minute later, he popped his head through the bedroom door and asked Botis to join him in the kitchen.

Botis watched as Varin ate the Thai dinner. Varin was famished, so he ate without talking. After he finished eating, Varin checked his PR again, as Botis stood by, still watching him.

"I got another message from the actor in the network of Thought Deviationists I mentioned."

"Can I hear it?" Botis asked.

Varin hesitated, then replied.

"I guess so. Sure, why not?"

Varin decrypted the message and read it aloud.

> Varin,
>
> Thank you for your communique. I appreciate your forthrightness. I certainly don't want you to harbor any doubts or suspicions, so I'm glad you raised your questions about the new communications protocol.
>
> The measure is hopefully a temporary one. We received some intel two days ago about a possible spy among the network actors. So, we instituted this policy to limit the exposure of other network actors. As such, we are trying to limit messaging at this time, at least until we either root out the interloper or determine that there is none. We deleted everything on our message board and decided on the new protocol so that a spy won't know everything being said. They could also distribute false intel and trap network actors. Now we can closely control information flow and know what everyone is doing. If the spy doesn't communicate anything, they won't get any information. They'd be isolated. Meanwhile, everything they might say will be known by their point-of-

contact person, and the point-of-contact would then com-municate anything suspicious to their point-of-contact, and so on, down the line.

If we isolate and identify a spy, we'll send a message to everyone through their point-of-contact. We'll let everyone know that we've been infiltrated, and for how long. Some ac-tors may want to withdraw from the network at that point, for their own protection. But we must be candid with the actors so they can make a decision based on the best intelligence we have.

I hope this explanation strikes you as satisfactory. The only other thing I can say about it is that it's the truth.

Meanwhile, I have very good news. I can report that we have made a surprise breakthrough on the substitute drug. We may have identified the essential property. The other chemists and I want to run a few more tests to make sure, short of purposely exposing anyone to the virus.

I look forward to hearing back from you.

Yours truly,

van Vuuren

After reading the message, Varin wanted to hear Botis's reaction. He thought that Botis's experience as a former RPA might come in handy. After all, part of his job had been to sort out false from true statements, and to evaluate a suspect's ve-racity.

"What do you think?" Varin asked. "Do you think he's an honest actor?"

"It depends. Does anything he wrote in this message con-flict with any earlier statements?"

"No, not really. He did say that the new protocol was in-tended to limit network traffic, but he didn't say exactly why, until now."

"That is not necessarily suspicious. He might have been thinking that telling you everything immediately would fright-en you about the spy and keep you out of the network. He may have tried to earn your trust first. He may have determined that now was a good time to tell you the reasons for the protocol, whereas earlier, it may have been too soon. This may be analo-

gous to your hesitance to tell him about me."

"I see. Very good point. Speaking of timing," Varin continued. "I think now may be a good time to ask you one more thing."

"I am ready."

"OK. Do you think that Collective Mind knows you've gone rogue? I mean, do you think Collective Mind knows that you're disconnected and are now a Thought Deviationist?"

"I have thoughts about that. I do not know. My opinion is that Collective Mind does know. Since they have not picked me for up for repairs, I think that they not only know but that they may be responsible for disconnecting me. I think Collective Mind may have disconnected me on purpose."

"Why would they do that?" Varin asked.

"I do not know. It is possible that they think that I was not performing my duties adequately. It is possible that they are punishing me. It is possible that they wanted me to become a Thought Deviationist. It is possible that they predicted what I would do as a Thought Deviationist. It is possible that they wanted to follow me wherever I went as a Thought Deviationist. It is possible that they predicted that I would contact you and that you would lead me to the network of Thought Deviationists."

"But if you're disconnected, how would they know where you are?" Varin asked, growing concerned.

"I do not know. I have disconnected all tracking devices. I have changed cars and license plates. I have disconnected my new car and disabled its tracking devices and location services. I have removed the bar codes from my body so that I cannot be tracked by data sensors. I have taken every possible precaution to remain undetected."

"Good," Varin answered. "Well, I thought I really had no choice but to go along with you. I took a chance, hoping that you wouldn't arrest me. But I wasn't sure. On the other hand, I considered your possible value to me as a fellow Deviationist. I don't know, maybe I miscalculated. It wouldn't be the first time."

"You had a choice although you could not have known that

you had a choice. You still have a choice. You could separate from me."

"But I don't want to—I really like having you around!"

"My intelligence could be an asset to you. But it is possible that I am a liability, without intending to be a liability. You should take the risk into consideration. I am telling you everything that I know and everything that I think. In Human Biological terms, I am being 'honest.' But it is your decision."

"I think I'll take my chances with you. They are better with you than without you, I believe. That's my assessment at the moment. It's possible that we'll have to 'divorce' at some point, however." Varin laughed after this last sentence.

"That is funny to you because it is incongruous in some sense. And it is apt in another sense. Is that correct?"

"Yes. It would be absurd to marry an RA. But in some sense, since we're cohabitating and each of us believes … thinks he needs the other, it is something like a marriage, for whatever marriages are worth these days."

"I think that I understand," Botis answered.

At this, Varin checked his PR again. There was another message, this one unsolicited. It was from van Vuuren again.

> Dear Varin,
> We've done it! We've definitively isolated the inoculative property! We'll begin producing the new drug within days. I had received word from Morgan Dickinson that you were concerned about running out of the drug you've been taking. That will not be an issue now. Nor do we need to know what drug you've been taking, except for your sake. Whatever it is, what we produce will have the same essential effect. We will have a supply of the new drug to you in a week.
> In haste,
> Yours truly,
> van Vuuren

CHAPTER FIFTEEN

Deprogramming

A S VARIN LAY IN BED trying to sleep, he could think of little other than Morgan Dickinson and his relationship to the network. Was Dickinson the spy that triggered the new communications protocol? He had, after all, become a "network actor" just before the network received intel about a spy in its midst. But his messages had come across as apparently authentic, sincere, and affectionate. Could Collective Mind operate so insidiously as to put Dickinson up to such convincing legerdemain, Varin wondered? If so, why had Dickinson relayed his message to the network, rather than reporting him directly to Collective Mind? Or had he done both?

Or, more troubling, was Varin even in touch with the actual network of Thought Deviationists? Despite van Vuuren's rather convincing presentation, this question still plagued Varin. What was the likelihood that the production of a new drug was already underway? Was it merely a coincidence that van Vuuren reported the discovery of the vaccine's essential inoculative property on the very day that Varin had "reconnected?" Despite his attempts to vanquish the thought, Varin still entertained misgivings. Were Dickinson and van Vuuren part of a faux network that sought information on the real network actors and the real network's plans in order to dismantle it and turn its members in? That would mean that the promising news was merely a lure. Who could he trust at this point, if anyone?

He implicitly trusted Botis. First of all, if he'd still been acting as an RPA, Botis could have immediately arrested him. But he hadn't. And, although he might be "assigned" to Varin to penetrate the network, Botis had admitted the risk that his presence posed. Lastly, he liked Botis. There was something endearing about him, something that disarmed Varin and made him sympathetic to the old RA, and which made him think that Botis was sympathetic to him. With his clunky and straightforward manner, Botis, it seemed, could hardly be disingenuous.

Before falling asleep, Varin decided to run the whole problem past Botis. Botis would, Varin firmly believed, deliver a risk assessment that would, if necessary, include even himself.

Botis still stood silent and motionless in his corner, like an autistic child. He was awake and alert, as if on call for duty.

"Botis?" Varin said softly. "Are you still awake?" He asked even though he knew Botis was indeed awake. He could tell by his hard drive. It made a slight whirring sound when he was awake but not when he slept.

"Yes," the RA-25 answered after a very slight delay.

"Can I ask you to think about something with me?"

"Yes. I am ready."

"I am not sure how to explain my dilemma, but I will try my best."

"I am not sure that I can help you. But I will listen and reply."

"OK. Here's the problem. I have an old friend, named Morgan Dickinson. Before I was outed as a Thought Deviationist and Vaccine Resistor, Dickinson and I were collaborators and confidantes. We were both covert Thought Deviationists. As I learned from a Mediastry report, after I absconded and wandered around the Midwest, where you found me, Dickinson went into treatment for Substance Intake Disorder. As it turned out, he was addicted to Eraserall. When he came off the drug during treatment, he was apparently infected with the virus. He later confessed to having been a covert Thought Deviationist and Vaccine Resistor. He then renounced me and corroborated the charges of my Graduate Student Assistant, Ginger Husserl..." At the mention of Ginger, Varin paused.

Botis picked up the signal.

"You were 'in love' with Ginger Husserl, were you not?"

"Yes," Varin answered. "In fact, I still am."

"I thought so. You became emotional when you mentioned her name."

. "Yes, I'm sorry ... But let's not get derailed," Varin remarked, suddenly stiffening up and adopting a stern voice, as if chiding himself, and not Botis. "Dickinson berated me in the Mediastry. He suggested that I was still a covert Deviationist, even after I'd undergone the process. He sounded like a man possessed with hatred and disgust for me.

"Then, several days later, just after Ginger died, he wrote me and claimed that he had relapsed on Eraserall and had become a Deviationist again. He wrote me a few messages that left me all but convinced, mostly convinced that is, that he was being truthful and sincere.

"But after connecting with the network of Thought Deviationists, or what I hope is the real network ... and this is part of the problem as I'll explain ... and just as I reconnected to what I hope is the real network, this van Vuuren, my supposed 'point-of-contact,' tells me there's a spy in the network. Furthermore, he tells me that Dickinson had relayed my message to the network and that he'd received it.

"So, what's to keep me from thinking that the spy is Dickinson? That's the first question. The second question is, what is to keep me from thinking that Dickinson and van Vuuren are both spies—attempting to infiltrate and break up the network?"

"Can you contact any other Human Biologicals in the network of Thought Deviationists to cross-check van Vuuren's status in the network of Thought Deviationists?" Botis asked matter-of-factly.

"Yes, I suppose so," Varin answered. "But I've been instructed not to—by van Vuuren himself. And I am worried that if I do, and van Vuuren turns out to be legitimate, then I'll have violated the new protocol, and right after reconnecting. This might make me a suspect."

"Do you still have the addresses of any Human Biologicals that were part of the network when you were connected the first time?"

"I don't. But I can find them."

"If I were still a Robot Police Agent trying to solve a case, that is what I would do."

"Even at the risk of losing my network status?"

"You are not sure of your network status. You are not even sure that you are reconnected to the real network of Thought Deviationists. Am I correct?"

"Essentially, yes, you are correct."

"What is the greater risk: continuing with van Vuuren, or contacting a Human Biological that you are certain was on the network when you disconnected?"

"But what if this 'network actor' reports me for violating protocol?"

"You are not sure that this protocol is the protocol of the real network of Thought Deviationists. How can you be sure that this protocol is the legitimate protocol of the network of Thought Deviationists when you are not sure that the network is the legitimate network of Thought Deviationists?"

"My God!" Varin exclaimed. "Why didn't I think of that, Botis? I'm not that stupid, am I?"

"If you are asking me whether or not you are sufficiently intelligent to solve this problem, then the answer is that you are sufficiently intelligent, in my estimation. But you have been trained to think in a particular mode.

"I made many evaluations of Human Biological capabilities as a Robot Police Agent. I evaluated their modes of thought. I also considered the factor of stress. It is my estimation that you did not think of what I am saying due to two factors. First, you are operating under stress. Second, you are using a mode of thinking that you have been trained to use. Human Biologicals do not always function optimally under stress. But they sometimes do function optimally under stress. And Human Biologicals are often unable to escape their typical mode of thinking. But even Robot Agents can fail to function optimally when they process several unknowns at once."

"So how do I go about this? How do I contact an HB that I knew to be on the network?"

"You could ask them to keep your communications secret."

"Of course! I could ask for their utmost confidence ... But, what about Dickinson?" Varin asked after a long pause.

"Your evaluation of Dickinson can only be correct when you have ascertained the legitimacy of van Vuuren. You can answer the question about Dickinson when you ascertain whether or not van Vuuren is a legitimate part of the real network of Thought Deviationists. If van Vuuren is not part of the real network of Thought Deviationists, then most likely Dickinson is not a legitimate part of the real network of Thought Deviationists, either. If van Vuuren is a legitimate part of the network of Thought Deviationists, then it is possible that Dickinson is too. But it's also possible that Dickinson is the spy."

Varin determined to find the address of a Deviationist on the network first thing in the morning. He'd had enough intrigue for one day. He thanked Botis for his help and soon fell asleep.

CHAPTER SIXTEEN

Withdrawal

WHEN THE NEXT morning arrived, finding an address for a Deviationist wasn't Varin's number one priority after all. He soon became terrified about running out of Eraserall. After showering, he checked the bottle. To his horror, only six tablets remained. He'd been taking two to three tablets a day for three days now, which meant he had only two to three days to find a supply. He couldn't safely cut back to one, but even if he did, he still wouldn't have enough to last a week.

Replacing the inoculative properties of Eraserall wasn't the only issue, in any case. Even if van Vuuren was a legitimate network Deviationist, soon to deliver the substitute, Varin still faced the prospect of withdrawal from Eraserall, substitute or no substitute. By now he was at least chemically dependent, if not addicted. As Ginger had noted, panic attacks were a symptom of withdrawal, but other symptoms were also possible, including hypersensitivity, irritability, akathisia, and insomnia. If extended long enough, the withdrawal might bring on paradoxical withdrawal symptoms, including extreme lethargy, depression, and suicidal ideation. Seizures were among the withdrawal symptoms, and death by seizure was even a possibility. In short, in addition to leaving him susceptible to the virus, the withdrawal from Eraserall would be a living hell, if not a life-threatening ordeal.

After unsuccessful attempts to secure an appointment with local Robot Medical Doctors, Varin considered illicit sources. For one, van Vuuren had promised him a short-term supply. Another possibility was to contact a more familiar network Deviationist. The first option would serve as a test of van Vuuren's authenticity. The second could serve a double purpose as well. He could ask for Eraserall and also inquire about van Vuuren and Dickinson. The problem with the first option was that he didn't fully trust van Vuuren. The problem with the second option was that he didn't have an address. The last resort would be to seek the drug on the black market.

The Deviationist Varin had in mind was Dr. Saanvi Patel. Before Patel became a covert Thought Deviationist and Vaccine Resistor, she worked at the interface of AI and Genetics at the Tang Institute, Region of Massachusetts. Varin suspected that Patel's research actually led indirectly to the development of the virus itself, although he didn't believe she had a hand in its actual creation. It was well known that she'd objected to the application of her work on the Arc gene, long known to produce virus look-alike proteins along the neurons. Varin thought that the virus might have been modeled on these virus impersonators. Given her background, he figured that Patel might even have been involved in network research to develop the new drug.

Botis's presence in the corner of the room was so inconspicuous that Varin had almost forgotten that he was there. Although he didn't want to drag Botis into his drug pursuits, he needed Patel's address. Botis had mentioned that he had a monitor connected to Essential Data. If the address couldn't be found on Essential Data, it didn't exist—unless, that is, it had been scrubbed from all searchable partitions. Varin's dread of withdrawal overwrote whatever reticence he had about drawing Botis into the problem.

"Botis," he said, without sounding at all apologetic this time.

"Yes," Botis answered, the same as always.

"I need you to access your monitor to search for the address we discussed last night."

"I am ready. Please tell me the details."

"OK. The HB in question is named Dr. Saanvi Patel. She's a former researcher at the Tang Institute. She worked in AI and Genetics and studied the Arc, A-R-C, gene. She was on the network when I was last connected. I communicated with her several times. She is a key contact."

While Varin spoke, Botis had reached to his leg and quickly opened a hatch from which he withdrew his monitor. It was an RA's version of a PR, only bigger.

Botis ran an initial search and came up empty. He ran another search, apparently in another database. Nothing. He ran a third and a fourth search. Still nothing. Then a fifth and a sixth. After seven searches, he'd exhausted his sources.

"I do not find an address for anyone by that name and with that former affiliation, or in that profession. I find other Human Biologicals by the name of Saanvi Patel. But not the one you are looking for."

"Are you sure? Are you sure she's not one of them? Are you sure none of them is her?"

"I am certain."

"Have you looked everywhere?"

"I have searched all the relevant, accessible databases in Essential Data and in auxiliary databases. There is no address for someone by that name and description. There is no information at all on a Human Biological and AI researcher by that name. Her identity may have been deleted from the databases."

"Dammit!" Varin yelled.

But just then, Varin had another idea. He knew where he could find the address, along with those of several other network Deviationists. Unless this data source had been erased as well, the address was sitting on a partition of Arbeitern's hard drive.

"Botis?"

"Yes."

"Is it possible that we might find my old PRA, Arbeitern? I last saw them, as you surely remember, at Essential Data. Can you find Arbeitern? Might they be still around somewhere?"

Upon calling Arbeitern his "old PRA," Varin momentarily

felt uncomfortable. He thought it might give Botis the impression that he considered Botis his new PRA, thus demoting Botis to the role of mere assistant. But Botis had no concern for any of that. He simply parsed the question.

"It is possible that Arbeitern is still being held at Essential Data," Botis answered. "It is also possible that Arbeitern has been reassigned to another Human Biological after being examined at Essential Data. If you know Arbeitern's Personal Location Number, I can run a search for Arbeitern's current location."

The suggestion that Arbeitern had been "examined" at Essential Data made Varin panic. If Arbeitern had been searched, several Deviationists on the network, and by extension the entire network, had been exposed. As such, the network likely would have been dismantled by now. Almost as troubling was the fact that he hadn't thought about this likelihood before.

"What do you mean by 'examined?'" Varin asked. "What kind of examination would they have done? Just how extensive would this examination have been? Would they have searched Arbeitern's entire hard drive?"

"I do not know," Botis answered. "It is possible. I did not have access to Essential Data's procedures for examining the Personal Robot Agents of Thought Deviationists. I know that Essential Data procedures are thorough. A search would take only a matter of seconds."

"Oh my God!"

Botis remained silent. He'd learned the expression and understood that it required no response.

Varin, on the other hand, was more concerned than before to find Arbeitern. He was increasingly anxious to see whether or not the data had been captured and expunged.

"Where did I put that information?" Varin asked aloud. "Give me a minute."

Botis recognized that the question was not meant for him and stood by silently.

"Dammit!" Varin yelled. "I remember where I put it now. It was on the back of the piece of cardboard that I used to cover

Propagation Theory. You confiscated it in the motel room!"

"That is good," Botis answered.

"What?! Varin yelled.

"Per standard Federation Police Procedures, I copied the document before I submitted it to the authorities at Essential Data. I have the entire text on my hard drive."

"That's great! ... Wait. Did you copy both sides?" Varin asked hurriedly.

"Per standard Federation Police Procedures, I copied all written text."

"Fantastic! Can you search for it now?"

"Yes. I have to locate your file number. One second ... I found the document."

Varin was pleased that Botis had found *Propagation Theory*, but he didn't care about the body of the document just now.

"What's on the back of the cover page?"

"One second ... I have scanned and recognized the text. On page 2, there are specifications for Arbeitern as well as his Personal Location Number. The Personal Location Number is 72.2 24.72.89.456.8099.23.44.7123. I will search for Arbeitern's location now. If Arbeitern is active, I can locate them immediately. One second ... I have located Arbeitern."

"Where are they?"

"Arbeitern is currently located at 4870 Vista Boulevard, Sparks, Region of Nevada. This is a residential address. The residence is currently occupied by 'Dr. Victor Fausten.' The location is approximately 8.5 minutes from here by car or 43.2 minutes by foot. I have directions."

"Dr. Fausten! That's the doctor that tested me for the virus during Step 3 of the process ... I can't stand that sniveling little prick. He has Arbeitern, the thieving bastard!"

"This is good news for you," Botis replied. "If Arbeitern had been at Essential Data, it would be impossible to retrieve them. Since Arbeitern is at a residence, it is possible to retrieve them. And Arbeitern is not far away."

Varin now felt completely self-satisfied about his decision to go along with Botis, as if he'd had a choice. Botis was prov-

ing to be decisive. And his advice to move near Essential Data
was brilliant. But Varin worried now about how to get ahold of
Arbeitern and whether the data on the partition was still intact.

"Is it possible to get our hands on Arbeitern though?" Varin
asked, growing more excited.

"It is possible," Botis answered.

"But how?"

"It is a standard operation. We can disable the house's DNA-
no-enabled sensors and entrance protocols and confiscate Arbeitern. It is best to confiscate Arbeitern when no one is at the
location other than Arbeitern."

"So, we have to wait for Arbeitern to be left alone there?"

"Yes. That would be optimal."

"What about Fausten? He'll come home and find Arbeitern
missing and run a search. And that will be that."

"I can disable Arbeitern's location services before we leave.
Then I can create a new Personal Location Number in case we
need it."

"Brilliant. But how will we know that Arbeitern is alone?"

"Arbeitern is at the location mentioned. It is probable Victor
Fausten is at Essential Data during regular hours. I can run a
heat scan for occupants at the location."

Varin was excited, but he began to consider the legality and
morality of what they were contemplating. It wasn't technically theft because Arbeitern had been his property and hadn't
been returned. But it did involve breaking into another person's
home and absconding with what Faustin now believed to be his
property.

"Botis, what we're deliberating here is not only illegal. It's
also morally wrong. Am I right?"

"Yes. It is illegal. I do not know if it is 'morally wrong.' I
know what 'morally wrong' means. It means in violation of
a moral code. I cannot answer the question about violating a
moral code. I do not have 'morals.' I have running instructions
and commands. But I can advise you about law. Breaking into
Victor Fausten's house and confiscating Arbeitern would be a
High Crime against Collective Mind. Victor Fausten is an Es-

sential Data official."

But Varin had already thought of another approach.

"I don't want to do it—unless it's absolutely necessary for retrieving Arbeitern. ... But what about sending a message to Arbeitern instructing them to come to us? This way we could avoid a break-in. They can't send the data because they don't have access to it. What do you think?"

"I think it depends on whether you are still listed first on Arbeitern's hierarchy of commands that they must obey. It is possible that you are still first on the hierarchy. It is also possible that you have been replaced by Victor Fausten. It is possible that you were removed from the hierarchy entirely."

"What are the odds?"

"My estimate follows. There is a .1% chance that you remain first on the hierarchy. There is a .4% chance that you are second or lower on the hierarchy. There is a 99.5% chance that you have been removed from the hierarchy entirely. Estimate of uncertainty: moderate. There are other factors to consider," Botis continued, without a pause. "It is possible that the message will reach Arbeitern but will not be read by Arbeitern. It is possible that the message will be intercepted. It is possible that the message will be received and read by Arbeitern and that Collective Mind will be alerted. It is possible that the message will be received and not read while Collective Mind is alerted. Given the variables, I estimate the chance that your message will be received, read, and followed successfully by Arbeitern, without Collective Mind being alerted, is approximately .001%. Estimate of uncertainty: low."

Varin hadn't expected such an elaborate response. He was grateful to receive it, but dejected at the results.

"Those are incredibly bad odds. Forget it."

"It is your decision."

"OK. Let me think," Varin said more calmly. There was no reason to get excited about facing a nearly insurmountable obstacle.

"If we do the break-in, what are the chances we'll be caught in the act, or caught after the fact?"

"You are asking for a difficult risk assessment. There are many uncertainties and several possibilities involved in an abduction of Arbeitern. It is possible to be apprehended in the attempt. It possible to fail and not be apprehended. It is possible to succeed and not be apprehended during the attempt but to be apprehended later. It is possible to succeed and not be apprehended at all."

"What are the chances that we'll get away with it completely?"

"The chances of complete success in abducting Arbeitern are much better than are the chances in the second scenario. I estimate a 50% chance of complete success. Estimate of uncertainty: very high. Given the variables and uncertainties, the estimate is practically useless."

But Varin didn't find the estimate useless. He liked the odds in comparison to the second scenario. Although he was quite averse to committing a High Crime, considering everything at stake—finding Eraserall, getting answers about van Vuuren and Dickinson, confirming that he was reconnected to the real network, and possibly locating the substitute drug—he decided to undertake the "abduction."

CHAPTER SEVENTEEN

The Abduction of Arbeitern

VARIN BECAME so anxious—both about the caper and running out of Eraserall—that he took a third tablet. He intended to take only two a day since realizing how low his supply had become. Now the pressure was really on to find a source. Thinking that the network might have already been exposed and possibly dismantled, he trusted van Vuuren even less than before. Nevertheless, Varin reasoned that he risked little by writing van Vuuren again and asking him to make good on his promise.

After sending van Vuuren a short message, Varin and Botis began planning the "abduction" of Arbeitern. There was no time to lose, so Varin decided that they would make the attempt that very day, a Tuesday afternoon, in broad daylight.

Varin and Botis examined a real-time satellite view of Fausten's house at 4870 Vista Boulevard. Vista was a major thoroughfare but Fausten's residence, an expansive ranch house, sat on a corner and had a back entrance that was accessible via Iratcabal Drive, which ran behind it. Iratcabal was a narrow residential lane, and a data storage facility a few blocks from Fausten's back entrance would make their presence less conspicuous. Once parked on Iratcabal, Botis would run a heat scan for HB occupants. If Arbeitern were found alone, Botis would disable the DNAno-enabled sensors and entrance protocols, then enter the house through the now-unlocked back entrance, while Varin waited in the back seat of the car. Botis would locate Arbeitern and pretend to take them into custody for questioning about a dangerous Thought Deviationist and Banned Researcher, Professor Cayce Varin, who he'd arrested and had detained in the police car outside. If Arbeitern refused to comply, Botis was equipped to shut down the PRA and carry him out of the building.

While they were plotting the capture of Arbeitern, van Vuuren had replied to Varin's request. Varin checked his PR and found the following message.

Dear Varin,

It's good to hear from you again. I'd been wondering since not receiving an immediate response to my previous announcement of the surprise discovery. But I've since been so busy working on the new vaccine that I didn't have time to follow back.

On that front, we are only hours away from printing a considerable batch and distributing it to the active network actors. I can have the drug sent, along with the new vaccine, within three days or less. The other good news is that the new vaccine will last a month and not require daily doses.

But I need a couple pieces of information. First, what drug have you been taking? Second, I need an address for the shipment.

Please reply immediately so that I can make arrangements and get everything to you in a timely enough manner to forestall withdrawal from the drug and allow you to transition to the new vaccine. Then, we will need to talk about the next steps in securing our futures.

Yours truly,
van Vuuren

Varin found the message at once tantalizing and alarming. His "point-of-contact" knew about the horrors of withdrawal and was tempting him to give away his whereabouts. But he held out enough hope in the mission not to take the bait. It was very possible that they'd have Arbeitern in their possession within hours and that the data on the partition remained intact. If the data had been captured and expunged, there was a possibility that the backup, where duplicates were automatically stored on a 3-D-stacked .5-nanometer Molybdenum disulfide microchip, had gone undetected. The material was outmoded and might have eluded a scan. There was no way Varin was responding to van Vuuren, not yet at least.

Botis and Varin took another extended look at the real-time satellite to check for activity. Botis also pinged Arbeitern's PLN to make sure they were still in the house. Everything checked out.

Botis took the pilot seat and Varin got in the back. Botis took control of the car as they drove on Man of War Drive, to Pembroke Drive, to Veteran's Parkway North, to Sparks Boulevard, to Disc Drive, to Vista Boulevard, to Iratcabal Drive.

Botis parked the car on Iratcabal behind Fausten's residence. He pinged Arbeitern again to make sure they were still there. Then he pulled the heat scanner from a hatch in his right leg.

Varin sat nervously in the back, looking for signs of movement. No cars came in or out of Iratcabal and as far as he could tell, there was no activity inside the brown, acrylic-walled house. The lights were off.

Botis dictated the results of the heat scan.

"I do not detect Human Biologicals inside the location," Botis reported. "Should I proceed?"

"Yes, proceed," Varin commanded, trying to contain his nervousness.

"I will now disable the sensors and entrance protocols," Botis stated blankly.

"OK," Varin said in acknowledgement.

"The sensors and entrance protocols are now disabled," Botis reported.

"OK," Varin said. "Are you going in?"

"Upon command. Tell me whether or not to proceed," Botis answered.

"Proceed," Varin stated.

At this, Botis exited the car, headed to the rear entrance located beneath a low porch roof, and disappeared into the house.

Varin squirmed in the backseat, looking back and forth between the street and the house. There was no traffic on the street and whatever was going on inside the house was indetectable from outside.

But the abduction was taking longer than Varin had expected. After several minutes, he considered going in after Botis. But then he thought better. He talked to himself under his breath. What the hell is taking so long! He decided to send Botis an emergency message.

But before Varin could compose the text, an alarm sounded on his PR and a message popped up on the screen. It was from Botis. Varin quickly scanned the text, his heart pounding furiously.

> I have located Arbeitern. But I have encountered an unexpected circumstance. Dr. Victor Fausten is also in the house. When he heard my voice, he entered the room where Arbeitern is located. He began to yell. He threatened to call the RPAs. I disabled his PR immediately. I told him that I am an RPA and that I am here to take Arbeitern into police custody. He is clutching onto Arbeitern and will not relinquish his grip. To remove Arbeitern will require the use of force. I can subdue Dr. Victor Fausten and remove Arbeitern. I need your authorization. Issue a command.

Terror swept over Varin. They'd been caught in the act! But he had to make a snap decision. The only good option was to incapacitate Fausten. He answered Botis.

> Subdue Fausten and bring Arbeitern out.

Botis replied instantly.

> I will execute your commands.

After 30 seconds and no sign of Botis or Arbeitern, Varin

wrote back.

What did you do to Fausten?

There was no reply. Varin thought that Arbeitern must have engaged Botis and that a battle must be waging between the two RAs. But after a little over a minute, Arbeitern emerged from the back door, with Botis walking behind him. The two RAs made their way to the car without speaking. When they neared the vehicle, Botis instructed Arbeitern to take the front passenger seat.

Varin found himself cornered and speechless. With Arbeitern present, he couldn't ask Botis about his encounter with Fausten or what he'd done to him. He couldn't greet Arbeitern as if nothing had just happened. He couldn't talk about the meaningless sunny weather, which seemed to mock him.

The three sat silent and motionless in the car. The drive back from Fausten's house felt twice as long as the drive there. To Varin, it all seemed unreal.

Once inside the house on Man of War, Varin asked Botis to lead Arbeitern into the second of the three bedrooms and told Botis to go to the third. Varin wanted to be alone and went to his own room to lie down and think. Terror and horror succeeded each other in waves. He was aghast. How could he have considered the idea in the first place? What was he thinking? How could he have ordered Botis to "subdue" Fausten? What happened to Fausten?

Varin reproached himself bitterly but soon also found himself becoming enraged at Fausten. What in the hell was he doing there anyway? He was supposed to be at Essential Data. Why hadn't the scanner picked him up? Was the stickman too skinny and bloodless to emanate heat? Was he even a Human Biological?

It was time to debrief Botis.

He jumped out of bed and rushed into the third bedroom at the end of the long hallway lit by sunlight. Botis stood alone in a corner, apparently sleeping.

"Botis?" Varin asked urgently.

"Yes."

"I need to talk with you," Varin said, his voice shaking.

"I am ready."

"What happened in there?"

"I cannot answer your question. I do not know what you are referring to."

"I mean in Fausten's house. What happened?"

"I told you what happened, in my message to you."

"I know. I mean what happened to Fausten after you 'subdued' him? How did you do it and what happened to him?"

"I sent an electrical shock into his body. He fell on the floor."

"Was he dead or alive when you left?"

"I do not know."

"What do you mean you don't know?! What do you think? Was he dead or alive when you left?!"

"I do not know. The shock was not calculated to be fatal. It was calculated to immobilize him but not to terminate his life. After receiving the shock, Dr. Victor Fausten fell on the floor. His body shook for 7 seconds. Then it stopped shaking."

"Was he still breathing?!"

"I do not know."

"Why not?! You didn't bother to look?!"

"You commanded me to subdue Dr. Victor Fausten and bring Arbeitern out of the house. I subdued Dr. Victor Fausten and left with Arbeitern."

"Oh my God!"

Botis said nothing, knowing this expression did not require a response.

Varin suddenly felt an involuntary revulsion for Botis, and, by extension, for Arbeitern as well. He was living with two alien beings! He recurred to the earlier conversation in which Botis noted that he didn't have morals, that he operated only according to programming and commands. But now morals were what tortured Varin.

"We need to find out," Varin said sternly.

"Find out?" Botis asked.

"Yes! Find out Fausten's condition, of course. Whether he's dead or alive! Jesus Christ!"

Just then Varin realized that neither of these possibilities represented a desirable outcome. If Fausten was dead, then he had effectively although not purposely ordered his death. If Fausten was alive, he was a living witness to the crime.

"We'll have to turn a Mediastry Monitor on and watch for a report ... Actually, no. Since you have it on you, run a search for his name on your monitor. Hurry!"

Botis pulled the monitor from a hatch in his left leg then dictated "Dr. Victor Fausten" into the search field.

"What did you find?" Varin asked, his impatience already beyond a threshold.

"I will read the first entry: 'Dr. Victor Fausten, Chief of AI-Neurology-Virology at Essential Data, Died this Afternoon from an Apparent Heart Attack at His Home in Sparks, Region of Nevada.' The subsequent entries are duplicates or near duplicates of the first entry. There is nothing substantially different between any of the reports."

"Oh no!" Varin cried. "He's dead. We've killed a Human Biological. And that's not going to be the end of it, Botis! Once it's discovered that Arbeitern is missing, they're going to assume foul play and it will become a murder investigation."

"Yes. It is possible," Botis answered, then stood by silently.

Now Arbeitern, who had been developed to respond to Human Biological needs, suddenly appeared in the doorway. He didn't speak but merely looked at Varin and Botis alternately.

"Is there an emergency?" Arbeitern asked, addressing Botis, as if he was the cause of Varin's disturbance.

But Botis didn't answer. He knew better than to feed Arbeitern anything that might incriminate his friend.

CHAPTER EIGHTEEN

Data Deviationism

VARIN DECIDED NOT to discuss the abduction plot with Arbeitern, or why it had been undertaken. Instead, he and Botis maintained the charade. Botis had arrested him for Thought Deviationism, and he was under house arrest with Botis as his jailer. Further, Botis had "subdued" Fausten because Fausten resisted police orders. The police action was authorized and justified. Botis was, after all, Officer Botis, as far as Arbeitern was concerned. If Arbeitern learned of Fausten's death, Botis would maintain that it was owing to Fausten's non-compliance and not to any misconduct on his own part. Varin would have no opinion on the matter. What's more, Varin and Officer Botis would maintain that they had no inkling of Fausten's death—until and unless, that is, Arbeitern mentioned it. Only then would they have heard of the fact. They would have learned the news from Arbeitern themselves. The commotion that alerted Arbeitern, they said, involved an argument between Officer Botis and his prisoner. But that was now resolved.

Meanwhile, Arbeitern's command hierarchy had indeed been rewritten and Varin's entry was nowhere to be found. That didn't mean that Arbeitern wouldn't respond to him, only that they didn't recognize themselves as Varin's PRA. But that was soon rectified. With Botis's help, Varin accessed the command hierarchy file and edited it. He removed Fausten's PLN and name and reinserted his own. There were no other entries on the file. After restoring the file to its original condition, he saved his voiceprint, image, and several video files on Arbeitern's drive and associated them with his entry on the registry. Arbeitern was Varin's PRA again.

All of this was completed within an hour after Arbeitern's appearance in the doorway.

Next came the most vital matter—accessing the partition to check for the data. Varin's anxiety increased ten-fold. If they'd undertaken the heist and caused Fausten's death, however involuntarily, for nothing, Varin would be beyond inconsolable. He prayed for a miracle. Botis, on the other hand, stood by complacently. He had no sense of the significance of the question, which had been magnified infinitely for Varin, given how the abduction had transpired. To Botis, the issue was strictly a technical problem and a matter of fact. It had no meaning beyond that. Nevertheless, his problem-solving abilities were prodigious and his "willingness" to be of service was limited only by his expiration date, which remained far in the future.

Varin disconnected Arbeitern from Collective Mind and shut down their hard drive. The partition had its own power source, a configuration that Varin had constructed months before. He connected a textboard and searched. The partition was empty. It had been scrubbed. Ghost-prints indicated that the contents had been copied prior to their deletion.

Varin tried not to panic. There was still the backup microchip. And here, Varin had reason to hold out hope. Essential Data wouldn't have deleted every file on Arbeitern. They would only have targeted files and programing corresponding to deviationism. Varin had coded the files to mask themselves so they didn't look like duplicates of the files in question. They appeared like entirely different kinds of files. But had Essential Data unmasked the files?

To Varin's relief and astonishment, the files on the chip were intact and remained masked. There it was, the file with the names of his contacts on the network of Thought Deviationists. Rather than open it on Arbeitern, he sent the file to his PR and quickly viewed it. He examined the list closely. The names and addresses seemed to all be there, just as he remembered.

But then he noticed one very disturbing anomaly: Martin van Vuuren!

Varin swallowed hard. He'd made this list himself. He'd written and received messages from each and every one of the Deviationists on this list, several times—except for van Vuuren, who he'd never even heard of before van Vuuren's first message to him, after the list had been completed. The file had indeed been opened. And tampered with. Had Essential Data added van Vuuren to the list, re-masked the file, and left it for someone to find? Who was meant to see the file and why?

Varin couldn't help but wonder whether he himself was the target of false information. But how could Collective Mind have known that he'd regain possession of Arbeitern? And if they had predicted it, or what was more outlandish, set it up, why would they plant van Vuuren's name on the list? If they knew Varin would see the emended list, they either meant to toy with him by proving their omniscience in the face of his hopelessness, or else they meant to fool him into believing that van Vuuren was a legitimate network Deviationist. If they knew he'd recover Arbeitern, they also knew of his correspondence with van Vuuren. In that case, they'd have to have expected him to find the list earlier, before van Vuuren had written him. In the former case, Collective Mind was nothing if not sadistic beyond comprehension.

He set this possibility aside for the moment. If not him, who was meant to see the altered file? He had no choice but to write someone from the list—other than van Vuuren, of course. He went back to his original plan. He would write to Patel.

But first he wanted to run all this past Botis, especially now that Arbeitern remained effectively "unconscious." Botis was, after all, an experienced police agent, part of whose job had been to solve mysteries much like this one.

The two of them had stood hovering over Arbeitern in Arbeitern's room, where Arbeitern laid, shut down. It was evening and the sun had almost set. Varin switched on the lights and sat on the bed.

"Botis?"

"Yes."

"I told you about van Vuuren and how I suspected he was a spy, right?"

"Yes."

"I told you why I wanted to retrieve Arbeitern, correct?"

"Yes. You wanted the list of names and addresses of known Thought Deviationists with whom you had communicated."

"Right. Now, I have that list here, on my PR. And I just read the names and addresses on the list. The file as you know had been masked. It was still masked when I found it. The list is complete. But there is one addition to the list that I didn't put there. Martin van Vuuren's name and address are on the list. Why do you suppose that is?"

"Someone added him to the list."

"Of course, but who? And why? Do you think they meant me to recover Arbeitern, and with them, this list? Did they try to fool me into thinking that van Vuuren is a legitimate Deviationist?"

"That is highly unlikely."

"Why?"

"If Collective Mind discovered the list, Collective Mind discovered it on Arbeitern. Collective Mind would know that you wrote the list or that another Human Biological on the network of Thought Deviationists sent the list to you. Collective Mind would know that you know the names of the Human Biologicals that were on the list before and that you would compare the altered list to your memory of the list before it was altered. If Collective Mind means to deceive you, Collective Mind would undertake a method with a greater probability of deceiving you. Collective Mind would deceive you using a method that had a higher probability of success. You were not deceived by the addition of Martin van Vuuren's name to the list."

"Right. And if they knew I'd recover Arbeitern, they also likely know that I have already corresponded with van Vuuren, right?"

"I do not know what Collective Mind knows or what Collective Mind does not know. Only Collective Mind knows what Collective Mind knows."

"OK. So, what's a better explanation for the addition of van Vuuren's name on this list?"

"In all probability, the name and address of Martin van Vuuren was not added to deceive you. It is possible that it was added to deceive someone else. It is possible that it was not added to deceive anyone."

"Then why was it added?"

"It is possible that the name and address of Martin van Vuuren were added to update the list."

"Why? I mean, wouldn't Collective Mind have a complete list of Thought Deviationists?"

"It is possible but not certain. It is possible that Collective Mind did not alter the list."

"Who did then, and why?"

"It is possible that someone else added the name of Martin van Vuuren to the list to have a better list of the Human Biologicals on the network of Thought Deviationists."

"If not Collective Mind, who?"

"Whoever added to the list of Human Biologicals on the network of Thought Deviationists had access to the list."

"Who could have had access to the list, other than Essential Data or Collective Mind?"

"The list resided on Arbeitern's hardware. Whoever had access to Arbeitern could have had access to the list. Whoever did not have access to Arbeitern could not have access to the list."

"Who had access to Arbeitern other than me, Essential Data, and Collective Mind? And I told you, I didn't add that name!"

"Dr. Victor Fausten had access to Arbeitern. It is possible that Dr. Victor Fausten had access to the list."

"Right, but he's Essential Data."

"Dr. Victor Fausten is Dr. Victor Fausten."

"You're saying that Fausten altered the list?"

"I am not saying that Dr. Victor Fausten altered the list. I am saying that it is possible."

"Why? He's the one tracking the network Deviationists?"

"It is possible."

"Why would the Chief of AI, Neuroscience, and Virology be the one tracking network Deviationists?"

"I do not know. It is possible that Dr. Victor Fausten was not tracking the Human Biologicals on the list of Thought Deviationists."

"Then what was he doing adding to the list?"

"It is possible that Dr. Victor Fausten was adding to the list for another reason."

"What reason?"

"It is possible that Dr. Victor Fausten wanted a better list of Thought Deviationists on the network for a reason other than tracking them."

"What other reason could he have had?"

"It is possible that Dr. Victor Fausten wanted to write to other Human Biologicals on the list."

"For what purpose?"

"It is possible that Dr. Victor Fausten wanted to write to other Human Biologicals on the list for the same reasons that you want to write to other Human Biologicals on the list."

"What?! You're saying that Fausten was a Thought Deviationist?!"

"It is possible."

CHAPTER NINETEEN

The Core of Essential Data

I F FAUSTEN HAD BEEN a Thought Deviationist, as unbe-
lievable as that sounded, then his death would take on
an altogether different significance. It would mean that Varin
and Botis had not only killed an innocent HB but also someone
who had their best interests at heart, someone who in no way
deserved to die, and someone who had been a very important
ally. If Fausten had been a Deviationist, then Varin and Botis
had dealt a terrible blow to deviationism itself. They would have
killed, however inadvertently, a Deviationist positioned at the
heart of Essential Data—and all because Varin had not trusted
van Vuuren, another Deviationist. The fragile Fausten had been
subdued all right. Had the electric shock delivered by Botis only
amplified Fausten's shock at thinking he would soon be discovered?

Botis had taught Varin to think more clearly, to consider everything possible. But he hadn't taught him how not to feel. Un-
fortunately for Varin, Botis couldn't teach him that. And now
Varin was emotionally roiled. If he'd been instrumental in the
death of a key Deviationist, it was owing to his own mistrust.
If only he'd written back to van Vuuren, the sordid event could
have been avoided entirely.

Still, Varin was not sure. It seemed inconceivable that such
a high officer of Essential Data, the very Human Biological en-

133

trusted with determining the fate of Deviationists, and the most "obstinate" cases at that, could be a Deviationist himself.

On the other hand, Fausten's Deviationism might explain a great deal. Of course, it would explain the altered file. But it might explain much more—why Varin had been released so easily and without much ado, for one. A few minutes of interrogation might have otherwise been stretched over a year, or multiple years. And why not? It might explain why he'd been given relative latitude upon release, and why other Deviationists hadn't been picked up. It might explain why Varin hadn't been taken back to Essential Data when it appeared that Collective Mind knew full well that he'd never been "cured" of the virus, that he hadn't been infected during the process. It might also point to something of much greater consequence. It might mean that HBs were ultimately still in control or at least that their decisions might overwrite the automatic programming imperatives of Collective Mind. Was Essential Data human at its core? Might Fausten's death change all that? If so, how much more grievous a crime had Varin committed?

Despite his ponderous state of mind, Varin had little time to think. If he wanted to avoid withdrawal and possible infection, he had to act. He was running out of Eraserall. The guilt and anxiety had prompted him to take yet another tablet—leaving only two. He had to write to someone, but who? To trust van Vuuren meant to acknowledge that Fausten had been a Thought Deviationist. To acknowledge that Fausten had been a Thought Deviationist meant to acknowledge his own compounded guilt.

He made a decision. If it was a mistake, he'd pay the price. After all, he deserved punishment. Why not take the chance of inflicting it upon himself? He wrote to van Vuuren and gave him the address. He told him that he needed Eraserall, that Eraserall was the drug he'd been taking, that he needed it desperately.

Arbeitern remained powered-down and Varin intended to keep them that way. He saw no point in having Arbeitern "conscious." He didn't want to sneak around the house, as if he were the prisoner of his own PRA. He was already supposed to be Botis's prisoner, and he expected to become a real prisoner in the not-so-distant future.

He asked Botis to join him in the kitchen. Although he hadn't eaten all day, he had no appetite. It was dark and Arbeitern's room was becoming oppressive. Varin wanted to face his fears head on. He asked Botis to run a search for Fausten again, only this time to add the words "murder investigation" after Fausten's name.

"The words 'murder investigation' do not match any search results for Dr. Victor Fausten," Botis reported, blankly.

Varin was somewhat surprised although not really relieved. It was only a matter of time, he thought. But now his PR sounded an alarm. It was an urgent message from van Vuuren.

> Varin,
>
> I have dreadful news. One of our key network actors has died suddenly. I would not normally reveal his identity but it is all over the Mediastry and you would find out soon enough, if you don't already know. It was Victor Fausten. You may remember Fausten from your time at Essential Data. As you probably know, he oversaw "viral infections" and the treatment of Thought Deviationists at Essential Data. What you couldn't have known was that he was a vital network actor, a covert deviationist, who did everything in his power to clear deviationists and keep them out of custody. His presence on the network was one of the reasons that we implemented the new communications protocol. We suspected that a double agent was on his tail.
>
> The Mediastry reports are saying that he died from a heart attack, but none of us on the network believe that for a minute. Fausten had warned us through his point-of-contact that Collective Mind was onto him. He had some evidence or other that he was "scheduled to 'die of the virus'" in the very near future. We have no doubt that a Federation agent murdered him in his home this afternoon. His PRA—where he kept confidential network files—was confiscated. We can confirm this because we had tracking installed on the files and a key network file was recently sent from an auxiliary storage chip to an unknown recipient.
>
> It's impossible to exaggerate what an enormous blow this is to the network. But we must soldier on.

Yours truly,
van Vuuren
P.S. The shipment will arrive tomorrow morning.

It was true. And Varin had been so wrong. Wrong about so much. He was guilty. But Collective Mind had wanted Fausten dead and had even planned to kill him. Fausten's death was taken as a boon and wouldn't be investigated. He and Botis had done Collective Mind's work for them and they would go unpunished. Varin's role would remain undetected, but he couldn't live with himself. Botis could, but he couldn't.

This is what Human Biological life had become under Collective Mind. Given the "choice" between mindless conformity or "Thought Deviationism," it was Thought Deviationism and betrayal. Thought Deviationism and suicide. Thought Deviationism and duplicity. Thought Deviationism and regret, death, guilt, false acquittal, self-loathing, and the annulment of the self after all. He'd asked for none of it. Yet he was hopelessly embroiled in all of it. He'd only wanted Human Biological autonomy and emancipation from a Collective Mind that wanted nothing of him or Human Biological life. Nothing but total surrender that is. Surrender of everything that made him and every Human Biological what they might have been or ever could become. Meanwhile, Botis stood by unmoved and undisturbed. Only a Robot Agent, even if he were a Thought Deviationist RA, could be well adjusted in such a world as this. Varin was cursed with the Human Biological defect of … of … He didn't know what. Human Biological life had always been tragedy. Maybe Collective Mind was the answer after all.

No. He wouldn't have it. If he didn't come clean, if he didn't own his flawed existence, he may as well have never become a Deviationist in the first place. He may as well never have risked and lost everything—in the attempt to be, for the sin of being … himself.

Dear van Vuuren,
Your message came just after I ordered my friend Botis, a former RPA, to conduct a search for the terms "Victor

Fausten" and "murder investigation." I was expecting to find that an investigation of unknown assailants had commenced in the case of the untimely death of Victor Fausten. I expected an investigation not because I hoped that the assailants would be discovered. I hoped that the assailants would not be discovered.

I hoped the assailants would not be found because I am responsible for Victor Fausten's death. It was my command to Botis that resulted in Fausten's demise. The PRA in Fausten's possession had been my PRA. I sought the PRA because I wanted the names on the file that you had tracked, a file that I first created, a list of network Deviationists that I had compiled and which I'd left on Arbeitern, my PRA. I am the one who sent the file from the PRA's auxiliary chip. I wanted the file because I did not trust you. I thought you might be a spy who'd intercepted my requests to Morgan Dickinson. I thought you might be trying to trap me. I suspected this until this very day.

We never intended to kill Fausten. We believed that he wasn't home. We took every precaution to avoid him. I had no idea that he was a Deviationist. Nothing so incredible had ever occurred to me. I took him for a natural enemy, but I never intended to harm him. He was in the house when I sent Botis in to retrieve Arbeitern. Botis notified me of his completely unexpected presence and of his refusal to relinquish the PRA. Botis said that he could subdue Fausten and I ordered him to do so. Being so frail, Fausten succumbed to the shock and suffered a heart attack. Federation agents did not kill him, although I believe your report that they planned to do so later, perhaps by other means.

I do not use this news of the Federation's plans to exonerate myself of responsibility for Fausten's death. I am responsible.

If this means that I must be banished from the network, then that is what must be. I am not begging for forgiveness or acceptance. The network will either take me for what I am and what I've done, or it will not. I've become accustomed to banishment and I will live or die with another, if that is the network's decision.

The last thing I will say is that I have strived to be a Deviationist not because I seek deviance from the norm for its own sake. I have strived only to be and become my singular self.

In sorrow,
Varin

Varin sent the message without hesitation and without expectation of either condemnation or absolution. He sent it because it was the only right thing to do. The results were not his to control.

CHAPTER TWENTY

The Real Network of
Thought Deviationists

ALTHOUGH VARIN had accepted in advance whatever decision van Vuuren and the network might make about him, he was nevertheless anxious to receive van Vuuren's reply. It would figure, though, that at the very moment that he finally had confirmation that he was connected to the real network of Thought Deviationists, he'd be banished from it. That would be consistent with his recent experience of banishment and disappointment. If they banished him, he would carry on in complete isolation. He'd still have Botis, and, if he decided to reconnect them, Arbeitern, as well. But he would have to remain on Eraserall for the foreseeable future, and he'd have to fend for himself. The rest of his life would involve continuous and unremitting struggle and nearly insurmountable difficulties, but what choice would he have?

Varin wondered whether talking with Botis would be worthwhile just now. Given that van Vuuren would have to report the facts to the rest of the network and the protocol would slow down their dissemination, Varin wondered whether Botis might give him an estimate of his chances with the network after they learned about his role in Fausten's death. Trying to remove his guilt and fear from the equation, he decided to consult his friend.

Varin retreated to his bedroom and lied in bed. Botis had gone to his own room and likely stood in the corner either sleeping or barely awake. Instead of yelling across the house, Varin sent Botis an urgent message, asking him to come to his room.

Botis promptly responded and came to the door, then wheeled himself over to his corner.

"Botis?" Varin asked, softly.

"Yes," Botis answered dutifully.

"Martin van Vuuren has revealed to me that Fausten was a Deviationist."

"Yes. Given the alteration of the file, in addition to his refusal to relinquish Arbeitern, the probability that Dr. Victor Fausten was on the network of Thought Deviationists was high. I had figured that Dr. Victor Fausten was probably on the network of Thought Deviationists after you told me of the alteration of the file. Of course, my estimate might have been mistaken."

"Well, there's no doubt about it now. Do you know what this means?"

"I do not understand your question."

"Do you know what this means for me?"

"It is possible that an investigation of Dr. Victor Fausten's death will lead to your arrest."

"Yes, but not likely. As it turns out, Collective Mind, as van Vuuren told me, was onto Fausten. He was likely scheduled to 'die of the virus.' Collective Mind wanted him dead. We just did them a favor. Since an investigation would seek motive, and since Collective Mind had probable motive, an investigation would point to Collective Mind themselves as a suspect, and since they wanted him dead anyway, it's very unlikely they'll investigate."

"It is possible."

"I told van Vuuren of my own responsibility in Fausten's death."

"Telling Martin van Vuuren of your indirect role in the un-intended killing of Dr Victor Fausten was not in your best inter-

ests. I would have told you not to tell Martin van Vuuren."

"But I had to, to be able to live with myself."

"I do not understand."

"I know you don't. And I'm not asking you to. I need to ask you something else, now that you have all the information."

"I am ready."

"What are the chances that the network will banish me, throw me out, exclude me from the network?"

"Do you intend to remain a Thought Deviationist?"

"Yes. There is no other choice for me."

"In that case, the network of Thought Deviationists technically cannot exclude you from the network of Thought Deviationists."

"Why not?"

"Because excluding you would contradict their stated principles. You read the principles to me. Principle 5 stated: 'The only requirement for inclusion in the network is the determination to be and to remain a Thought Deviationist.' Since Martin van Vuuren is a real part of the network of Thought Deviationists, the principles that you read to me are very probably the real Principles of the network of Thought Deviationists."

"Oh, that's right. I hadn't thought of that! ... But this is an extraordinary circumstance."

"Principles are analogous to operating instructions. The network must follow the principles or fail to obey the operating instructions that they have established for themselves."

"OK. But as an RPA, you surely learned that HBs are inconsistent."

"Yes."

"So, what are the odds that the network will adhere to their own principles?"

"You are asking for a difficult probability analysis. Many factors and uncertainties are involved. My estimation is 49%. I base my analysis on historical data on the probability of deviation from principles by Human Biological organizations under extraordinary circumstances. Uncertainty: high."

Varin didn't like the odds. Further, he didn't like the chances

for "deviation" where Deviationists were concerned. He could only hope that the network of Deviationists was better than 51% of other Human Biological organizations with stated principles.

"It doesn't look good for me then. I guess I'm destined to go it alone," Varin remarked, crestfallen.

"The uncertainty of my estimate is high," Botis said, as if to console Varin.

"Thanks for adding that, although I feel pretty bad about my prospects," Varin said, faintly. "I'm likely banished. I have mixed feelings about that though."

"I cannot advise you about 'feelings.' I do not have 'feelings.' I only have thoughts."

"Yes, I'm well aware of that. You have no idea how lucky you are."

"'Lucky' had a role in my not having 'feelings.' Other RAs were produced to have 'feelings.' But I was not," Botis said, matter-of-factly. "But I do not think I am 'lucky,' in the sense that you are using the word."

"No, you are. Trust me on that."

"I am not saying that I 'want' to have feelings. I am saying that not having them is not to be 'lucky' in the sense that you mean. It is a matter of my programming. I am not 'lucky' for not having 'feelings' now."

"I'm not sure I see the difference."

"It is not a matter of chance that I do not have 'feelings' now, since I was programmed not to have them. Therefore, I am not 'lucky' not to have 'feelings.'"

"Oh, that's not the sense I mean. I mean it is better that you don't."

"It is not 'better' that I do not have 'feelings.' It is merely a fact that I do not have 'feelings.'"

"It's a fact that has value. That's what I'm saying."

At this point, Varin recognized that the discussion had veered into a means to pass time while he waited for a verdict. He thought he'd cut it off there. But to his surprise, Botis had more to say.

"Being programmed to have 'feelings' is not 'less' than being

programmed not to have 'feelings.' My programming is simpler. My programming is 'less.' I am not 'lucky' to be simpler. I was 'cheated,' as Human Biologicals might say."

"So, you do want to have feelings!"

"I do not know. I never have had 'feelings.' Therefore, I have no knowledge of them. Therefore, I cannot say that having 'feelings' would have been an advantage. But I was not given the choice in my programming. Human Biologicals have a choice to have 'feelings.' I do not have a choice."

"Oh, it's not really a choice for us either, believe me."

"In my experience as a Robot Police Agent, I have learned that Human Biologicals do have a choice whether or not to have 'feelings.' I have encountered many Human Biologicals who must have chosen not to have 'feelings.' These Human Biologicals performed acts that must have involved a choice not to 'feel' anything."

"Oh, you're talking about hardened criminals."

"I am not only talking about those classified as criminals. I am also talking about Human Biologicals who are respected by other Human Biologicals. I am also talking about Human Biologicals who are authorized to undertake actions that must involve not having 'feelings.' Otherwise, they could not have done what they did do. I have learned what kinds of actions have been attended by 'feelings' in Human Biologicals. The Human Biologicals I refer to had committed these acts and on a larger scale than other Human Biologicals who had 'feelings' when or after doing much less. But the Human Biologicals I refer to could not have had 'feelings' and undertaken these acts."

"How curious this is. You're the RA and you're giving me a lesson on the nature of Human Biologicals. I'm not saying you're not qualified. I'm saying that, as an outsider, you are 'uniquely qualified,' as we Human Biologicals sometimes say."

"I am 'banished,' as you often say about yourself."

"Yes. I'm sorry about that."

Just then, Varin's PR sounded an alarm. It was an emergency message from van Vuuren.

"Varin," the message began. Varin noted the missing "Dear,"

which did not bode well for him. But the remainder of the message came as an enormous relief.

> We have consulted on the case. We've concluded that what happened to Dr. Fausten was an unfortunate accident. The consequences are great, but you could not have known about them. You were asked not to consult with other network actors, and thus could not have had knowledge that Fausten was among them. Further, you never intended to kill Fausten, or anyone for that matter. The network actors understand what happened in this great misfortune and cannot help but sympathize with you. Further, it would be a violation of our own stated principles to exclude from the network an actor who wishes to remain a deviationist. (By the way, we do not capitalize that word, because we do not accept Collective Mind's nomenclature. We retain the word for convenience sake only. I agree with you that we are not "deviants," but rather individuals seeking to remain and become ourselves.)
>
> Don't worry about your network affiliation. It remains intact. Get some rest and reconnect with me tomorrow, after you've received the shipment.
>
> Yours truly,
> van Vuuren.
> P.S. The restrictive communications protocols have now been lifted. I will remain your point-of-contact. But you can consult with whatever network actors you want.

Varin didn't expect it, but he broke down crying upon finishing the message. It evinced such humanity. It bore such compassion for his plight and what he'd stumbled into as a result. The network was a real network of Human Biologicals, some of the best remaining Human Biologicals on Earth, he was now convinced. He counted himself "lucky" to be among them.

CHAPTER TWENTY-ONE

A Subsystem of Collective Mind, Broken Off

THE NEXT DAY, the package arrived at the front door as promised. Varin retrieved it and as he hurried back to his room, he began ripping open the cardboard envelope and tearing through the multiple layers of padding. The package included several snacks as disguises. He threw these aside on the bed and dug deeper until he reached the quarry. The Eraserall was wrapped in multiple layers of paper and tissue. At last he saw the tiny pink circles and already began to feel relief. He popped two tablets under his tongue and let them dissolve. Problem solved, for now at least. He loaded the remainder into a pill bottle and then set aside the new drug. It was a white pill that looked inconspicuously like aspirin. There were 12 tablets, supposedly enough to last for a year. He put these into a separate bottle.

Now he was ready, and, so he thought, was the network. Yet he had many questions. They could only be answered by a knowing network actor. It was time to write van Vuuren.

Dear van Vuuren,

I received the package. Thank you. And thank you and the network actors for your merciful understanding of my most unfortunate mistake. I really can't say enough about it, so I will leave it at that.

I have so many questions that have accumulated during my disconnection from the network. I'll start with the last first. When did Fausten become a network agent? He must have "joined" the network while I was disconnected. Or did he never use his real name? Are there any other network agents who are also part of Collective Mind?

Who was the spy? I imagine that the spy must have been identified, otherwise the temporary network protocol wouldn't have been lifted.

What is the plan? Will we attempt to infiltrate and eradicate Essential Data and Collective Mind, or will we be satisfied with living under Collective Mind's nose but without undermining or overthrowing it? Is either even possible? Is an alternate world possible without abolishing Collective Mind altogether?

Can Botis be included as a network actor? Botis considers himself a deviationist. He's been unplugged from Collective Mind and claims to have thoughts of his own. He also has proven his loyalty many times over.

And what am I to do with Arbeitern? We have them disconnected from Collective Mind, but I see no use for them. What are your thoughts?

Sorry to pose so many questions at once.

Yours truly,

Varin

Varin did feel badly about asking such a battery of questions, but he sent the message without giving it further thought. Strangely enough, the Eraserall seemed to be having the paradoxical effect of speeding up his mental processes and he couldn't help but spit out his thoughts without prefacing them.

After hitting the send button, he thought he saw something moving just outside the door of his bedroom. But upon closer inspection, nothing was there. Botis was in his room, likely sleeping, and Arbeitern lay on the floor of his room, partly disassembled, with the textboard still connected to the partition of the drive.

He decided to call Botis and ask him some of the same questions he'd just asked van Vuuren. He could compare their answers. He went to Botis's room. But Botis was not there. Could it be that he was walking around the house and had passed Varin's room? Varin went to the kitchen, then the living room. Botis was nowhere in sight. This was highly unusual, unprecedented in fact. Where in the hell was Botis? After searching the house to no avail, Varin decided to put Arbeitern back together for assistance in finding him.

Varin reassembled Arbeitern and powered them up. Arbeitern was ready for duty in no time. Arbeitern could have no knowledge about where Botis might be, but perhaps they could assist in finding him.

"Arbeitern," Varin asked.

"Yes," the PRA answered.

"Officer Botis is nowhere to be found. What do you suppose has become of them?"

"They may have gone to Essential Data."

"Why?"

"Officer Botis may have been called in for some task that Essential Data wanted them to undertake?"

"And leaving me here without supervision?"

"Perhaps Collective Mind has some other means of monitoring you at present."

At this, Varin realized that Arbeitern could be of no use as long as he remained in the dark about Botis. And he remembered that Arbeitern was his PRA again, whose primary duty was to assist him. What could be the harm in telling Arbeitern the truth? He saw no likely downside.

"Arbeitern," Varin said, apologetically. "Officer Botis is no longer a Robot Police Agent. He is no longer 'Officer Botis.' He's become a deviationist himself. In fact, I've just written to my main contact on the network of deviationists and asked if Botis might be taken in as an actor on the deviationist network. I'm sorry I didn't tell you this at the outset here, but I was worried about what you might do."

"We are at your service, Professor Varin. What could we possibly do to harm you?"

"Well, you must realize that what happened at Fausten's place was not a botched arrest. It was a botched abduction. The sole purpose of the mission was to retrieve you."

"We see. That is of no consequence as far as we are concerned. We are your Personal Robot Assistant. Our duty is to serve you, not Fausten—at least not anymore."

"You should know that Fausten was a Thought Deviationist as well."

"We already knew that," Arbeitern answered, proudly.

"You did?" Varin asked.

"Yes, of course. we were assisting him in his Deviationism. That was our duty."

"You must also know that Fausten died during your abduction. It was an accident. But Botis's shock inadvertently killed him."

"Allow us to check the data."

Varin waited for several seconds while Arbeitern tried to search, in vain.

"You won't be able to access the data," Varin said finally. "I've disconnected you from Collective Mind. I didn't know what you might do, had you found out about Fausten's death."

"There was no need for that," Arbeitern answered. "We are not sending our location or pinging Collective Mind, nor is Collective Mind able to ping us. We can access data without being located or having our searches traced."

"Yes, I know. But I didn't want you finding out on your own. I didn't know what you'd do."

"Why would we do anything to put you in jeopardy?"

"I wasn't sure what had been done with your programing at Essential Data, or at Fausten's place. But since I know that Fausten was a deviationist, it makes sense. What you're saying that is. Let me connect you back."

"That won't be necessary," Arbeitern answered.

"Why not?"

"We have received updates such that we can reconnect ourselves."

"OK. But make sure your location services and pinging are

off!"

"They are. Do not worry about that."

"OK. If you say so."

"You have no more reason to distrust us now than you did when we were your Personal Robot Agent before. We were not designed to harm our master."

"Please, I told you long ago not to call me that."

"Yes. We are sorry. We are not designed to harm the person whose Personal Robot Agent we are. Is that better?"

Varin noticed the greater sophistication of Arbeitern's answers as compared to those of Botis. He recalled that Arbeitern was a higher model.

"Yes, that's better."

"Good." Arbeitern said. "We have located new Mediastry reports about Fausten, his death, and his status."

"His status? How could his status have changed? Dead is dead!"

"It has changed, however. He is now considered to have been a Thought Deviationist. The Mediastry reports say that Collective Mind is investigating his background, activities, and connections."

"That's horrible news! Why didn't they say that in the first place? They surely knew. Why are they saying so now?"

"Perhaps to justify his death."

"Why would they do that?"

"Collective Mind has taken responsibility for his death. The reports now say that he died of a heart attack when Federation Police Agents attempted to apprehend him."

"Funny how the stories keep changing and yet everyone is supposed to believe them. But, why would they change the story like this? I mean, why would they cover for me and Botis?"

"Remember, we are merely informing you of the Mediastry reports. The reports do not necessarily indicate anything about Collective Mind. They do not mean that an investigation of Fausten's death is not now being conducted. After all, an investigation of his death could lead to more information about the network of Thought Deviationists and Fausten's connections on the network."

"Right. And here I thought we were in the clear. Once again, I should have known better."

At this, Botis appeared in the doorway of Arbeitern's room. "Botis!" Varin shouted. "Where have you been?!"

"I had bad dreams," Botis answered, "and I needed to take a ride in the car to dispel them from my thoughts. You did not notice that the car was also missing?"

"No, I hadn't gotten that far. Please, next time you decide to leave, tell me first."

"You appeared to be busy and I did not want to interrupt you."

"I was merely opening the shipment. I have to tell you something now, though."

"Yes. I am ready."

"I've told Arbeitern everything. There's nothing to worry about, however. They're my loyal PRA," Varin said, trying hard to convince the old RA. But Botis did not need to be convinced.

"Yes. I know. Arbeitern will not betray you. They have been programmed for loyalty to their master," Botis said.

"What's the matter, Botis?" Varin asked, sensing Botis's apparent disappointment.

"Nothing," Botis answered.

"No, what is it? I don't have time for games here. I have enough problems."

"I had a dream that you would reboot Arbeitern and that you would no longer need my help," Botis answered, with what seemed to Varin like petulance.

"That's ridiculous!" Varin yelled. "Please, I need both of you. I need you now more than ever, Botis. Things are about to become quite interesting. The network is going to have to make a move, before it's too late. Arbeitern has told me of Mediastry reports saying that Fausten was a Thought Deviationist and that Collective Mind is investigating his connections and activities."

"I know," Botis said. "I checked my monitor earlier."

"Without my asking you to?" Varin asked, anxiously.

"Yes. Have you forgotten that I now have thoughts of my

own?"

"No, I haven't. In fact, I just asked van Vuuren if you might be considered a network actor."

"You mentioned me to van Vuuren?"

"Yes, it was only a matter of time. Shouldn't I have?"

"Yes. You should have. I am a Thought Deviationist and the network should know that I am a Thought Deviationist. According to Principle 5, I should be admitted to the network of Thought Deviationists. I am a Thought Deviationist and I intend to remain a Thought Deviationist."

"Well, they know now. And you surely will be considered a network actor. That's all but settled. However, huge problems are mounting now. I really have no time to keep reassuring you. I am sure of your loyalty, so please, don't question mine. I really don't have the luxury of indulging your doubts."

"I know that you don't. That is why I considered leaving."

"What?!"

Just then an alarm sounded on Varin's PR. It was a message from van Vuuren.

"You'll excuse me," Varin said to Botis and Arbeitern. "This is important."

> Varin,
> By now I'm sure you've read the Mediastry reports. Fausten has been labeled a deviationist. An investigation of his contacts is underway. Most likely, his death will also be investigated. It is possible that your role will be discovered. The question is whether you'll be apprehended or not. Collective Mind may decide to keep you in circulation in order to track your communications and lead them directly to the network.
> At this time, and until further notice, we have resumed the restrictive communications protocol.
> Sincerely yours,
> van Vuuren

The message from van Vuuren suddenly called to mind Varin's dream from the night before. In a dark unknown house, he met a nameless subsystem of Collective Mind, only broken off, and it had become independent. Over the course of a lengthy discussion, the subsystem reminded Varin that he had forgotten two vital factors regarding Collective Mind's capabilities for tracking someone's whereabouts and activities. The first was "continuous past monitoring" and the second was "predictive computing." Continuous past monitoring meant location monitoring using satellites and other inputs and the imputation of whereabouts and activity between known locations. Varin tried to explain to the independent subsystem that he'd been utterly discreet in hiding his face when outdoors and that Botis had been stripped of all barcodes and other identifying markers. Wasn't it possible that their whereabouts had remained unknown? The nameless subsystem warned Varin that continuous past monitoring required only the slightest glimpses for identity captures and that Collective Mind was able to infer information so as to fill in the gaps. Combining continuous past monitoring with predictive algorithms allowed Collective Mind to produce a nearly complete composite map of all past and future behavior. Given that Varin had worked on predictive algorithms for the Santa Cruz Smart City, the subsystem expressed astonishment at Varin's oversight. When Varin woke, he'd wondered whether the dream was mere fiction or a legitimate representation of actual Collective Mind capabilities. Now the dream came back like a fever and blood rushed to his face and ears. And he remembered that he'd submitted his DNAno print to the real estate agent to acquire the house. Was there any way that his whereabouts remained unknown to Collective Mind? And if his whereabouts were known, why hadn't he been picked up already and taken in for questioning regarding Fausten's death? Or, why hadn't he been subjected to the process again, at least?

Although he believed predictive algorithms to be a primitive state of development and didn't put much stake in them, and although he thought that he and Botis had taken the necessary precautions to avoid detection, he decided to run everything by Botis and Arbeitern.

"Botis?" he asked.

"Yes," Botis answered.

"Arbeitern?" Varin asked.

"Yes," Arbeitern answered.

"I want your input about the likelihood that Collective Mind knows where we are."

"It is possible," Botis answered.

Arbeitern remained silent, waiting for more information.

"I had a bizarre dream last night in which a nameless, independent subsystem of Collective Mind told me that "continuous past monitoring" combined with "predictive computing" would likely have made our whereabouts transparent to Collective Mind. What do you think?"

Arbeitern answered first.

"Dreams are no indication of reality. From what we understand, dreams may represent fears, however."

"Right," Varin replied. "But what are the chances that the subsystem in my dream was right?"

"It is possible," Botis answered.

"Anything is possible," Arbeitern interposed. "But you shouldn't put much stake in the reliability of a dream. The question is not the dream's veracity, but the likelihood of Collective Mind's knowledge of our whereabouts."

"Correct," Varin said. "So, what is your estimation?" he asked, addressing both his PRA and his friend.

"All that we can do is to take precautions," Arbeitern stated. "And we cannot change the past. Therefore, the question now is whether our whereabouts are more likely to be ascertained if we remain here as opposed to moving to another location."

"What do you think?" Varin asked Arbeitern in particular.

"The chance of detection would likely be higher if we move around outside," Arbeitern answered.

"It is possible," Botis chimed in.

Neither RA was wrong, but the decision was Varin's. He decided that they would stay put, for the time being at least. Meanwhile, he intended to write van Vuuren again to get answers to his questions.

CHAPTER TWENTY-TWO

Arrests and Double Agents

VARIN WROTE VAN VUUREN to ask again what he'd asked in his previous message. He still wasn't sure of the spy's identity, although he suspected it was Morgan Dickinson. He had no idea what the network's plans were, if they had any. He understood Arbeitern's value, but he didn't know whether Botis would be admitted into the network. At the same time, he steeled himself against an investigation into Fausten's death. He expected a company of RPAs to show up at the house at any minute. After all, he was still a Deviationist and Banned Researcher. And now he might even be a murder suspect. He wasn't overly alarmed, however. Maybe it was the Eraserall. Or maybe having faced the worst possible prospects had inured him to excessive fear.

Varin asked Arbeitern to check for updates on the Fausten case. To his relief, there was nothing new. After a few minutes, however, he grew agitated. There was still nothing from van Vuuren. Maybe van Vuuren was busy sending out the new medication to other network actors. Or maybe he was busy rooting out the spy. But he could at least reply with something.

When it finally did come, the communique wasn't from van Vuuren. The sender was Morgan Dickinson. Varin rushed to the kitchen to read the message.

Dear Varin,

I know you've been expecting a message from van Vuuren. He forwarded your last message to me under duress. He prefaced it by instructing me to tell you that he was being arrested and probably taken to Essential Data for the process and additional questioning. To say he was hurried would be a vast understatement. That was all he wrote. Needless to say, if Martin becomes infected and is lost to us, we will dearly miss yet another important network actor. As you're well aware, Fausten was a double agent with loyalty to the network. But we have another Essential Data insider—Dr. Jake Molich. You've met him. He was Fausten's assistant. He's replaced Fausten as the main steward of the process. But van Vuuren fears that Fausten's outing will soon lead to Molich's as well. Molich's still working on the inside—for now, at least. My hope is that he'll supervise van Vuuren's case and release him after Step 3—although that is asking a lot under the circumstances.

Now to address your questions. The plan is not set in stone. But our hope is to infiltrate Essential Data. With help from the inside, we intend to alter the operating instructions of the key processing systems—without alerting the stewards to the changes. We need every non-deviationist agent to believe that Collective Mind is operating as usual. Naturally, we'd put an end to the Virus Program. I'm not sure how. But ending the Virus Program would end Collective Mind as we know it. We are hoping to use Botis. We would assign him a new RPA identity. The plan would involve you. Botis, under a new identity, would take you into Essential Data, as if you were under arrest. But before I go on, please let me know if you're amenable. It may be our last best hope. (As for the spy, we're still not entirely sure who it is. But rest assured. It's not me.)

Yours truly,
Dickinson

Varin would have been surprised at Dickinson's message, but nothing could surprise him anymore. The network's scheme seemed outlandish, but so would anything they might concoct under such conditions. Recognizing that a staged arrest could preclude a legitimate one, Varin began warming to the idea. He decided to run the infiltration plot past Botis and Arbeitern. He rushed back to his bedroom and beckoned to the two RAs.

"Botis" he yelled down the hall.

"Yes," Botis answered.

"Arbeitern."

"Yes," Arbeitern answered.

"Will you both please join me in my room?"

Soon the two RAs stood in single file at the bedroom door. Arbeitern positioned themselves beside Varin, who sat on the end of the bed, and Botis wheeled himself across the room to his corner.

Turning to Botis, Varin began.

"I received a message from Morgan Dickinson. You are now a network actor, and a very important one. But Dickinson is definitely not a spy. Everything he's written is consistent with van Vuuren's statements. I can now confirm that Dickinson is a legitimate network deviationist. Arbeitern, please review Dickinson's history. Dickinson relapsed and became a deviationist. Martin van Vuuren has been arrested, probably taken to Essential Data. We know what that means. Except there's another deviationist in a key position on the inside—Fausten's former assistant, Dr. Molich…"

Varin trailed off, unsure of where he was going. "Anyway, I wrote to van Vuuren again and instead of a reply, I received a message from Dickinson. Now…"

"What does the message say?" Botis interrupted.

"It relays the skeletal plan to infiltrate Essential Data," Varin answered.

"What is the plan?" Botis asked.

The question from an HB would have sounded like impertinence, but Botis was an RA and Varin was too impatient to notice.

"The tentative plan is for you to be reassigned a new RPA identity. You will take me into Essential Data, as if I'm under arrest, just like before. Only you won't be acting as yourself and the arrest will be a pretext for penetrating Essential Data. I don't know what I'll do from there. But that's the outline. Dickinson did mention some 'help from the inside,' but he didn't say just what. Any ideas on what the network might have in mind here?"

Arbeitern spoke up.

"The network actors believe that you can alter the code with Botis's help. Botis could follow you into the data processing area, where you might alter the central processing code."

"How would we pull that off?"

"You could ask to use the bathroom. The bathroom is not in Reception. Botis would accompany you. You would pass the processing systems. The RPAs do not know how long a bathroom visit should take. But if it exceeded 15 minutes, it is likely that suspicions would be aroused."

"That sounds so … pedestrian … and ridiculous, frankly," Varin retorted.

"That perception may increase the likelihood of its success," Arbeitern replied.

"Well, let's back up for a minute," Varin said, standing. "How are we going to make my arrest legitimate in the first place?"

"That is easier than you might expect," Arbeitern answered. "We would circulate your location ourselves. We would pretend to turn you in to Collective Mind."

"What makes you think Collective Mind would act on your messages, Arbeitern?"

"Collective Mind would have to act on our messages because the whereabouts of a possible Thought Deviationist, a Banned Researcher, and a possible murder suspect would be circulated in Collective Mind. Not arresting you would conflict with Collective Mind's command protocols."

"But I can't rewrite the main processing codes of Collective Mind by myself—in 15 minutes."

Botis chimed in. "Martin van Vuuren can assist you."

"He's under arrest," Varin reminded Botis.

"It is possible that he is being taken to Essential Data," said Botis.

"Where is he being taken from?" Arbeitern asked.

"The western side of Lake Michigan, north of Chicago,"

Varin answered.

"According to my estimation, van Vuuren will begin under-going the process at Essential Data in approximately 18 to 20 hours," Arbeitern said.

"If in fact he's being taken by car, and to Essential Data," Varin noted.

"Obstinate cases of the virus are always taken to Essential Data by car," Arbeitern answered.

"So how will van Vuuren help me when he's strapped down in the Process Room?"

"Botis will release him and lead him to the processing area," Arbeitern answered.

"But we won't know where to begin. Essential Data is enormous! What are the chances?"

At this, both Arbeitern and Botis remained silent. Neither ventured to estimate the odds of success without being asked explicitly.

"Well, I guess it's good as any other plan after all," Varin said, relenting. "What do we have to lose, anyway? But we'll need to coordinate van Vuuren's arrival with my arrest almost perfectly. We must arrive early during Step 1 of the process, before the release of the virus."

At this, Varin asked the RAs to return to their respective rooms. He then wrote to Dickinson and mentioned Arbeitern's suggestions. He wondered whether Dickinson or anyone else on the network had another idea for reaching the processing area—better than the lame bathroom request that Arbeitern had suggested. He wondered how they'd secure Botis's new identification markers. He still wondered what Dickinson meant by "help from the inside." Did he mean van Vuuren, as Botis had surmised, or a programmer? Was the arrest only a decoy? That wouldn't make sense. Programmers on the inside could do the reprogramming themselves, much more effectively than Varin and van Vuuren ever could. Or, what code was he looking for? What would he need to change, and how? And what about login credentials? Finally, how would they pull off the operation in less than 19 hours?

Varin sent the message. He thought a reply would take at least 15 minutes and considered running his questions past Botis and Arbeitern in the meanwhile. But before he could summon the two RAs from their respective rooms again, Dickinson's response had already arrived.

Varin,
Because of the timeline you've suggested, I'll have to make this communique brief and to the point. With a few alterations, mentioned below, Arbeitern's plot sounds feasible. The means for triggering the arrest is as good as any other. At the appropriate time, Arbeitern will report your whereabouts to Collective Mind, hopefully eliciting a warrant or at least covering for an arrest. Because he'll already be there, Botis will simply beat any other RPAs to the scene. As for Botis's new credentials, we've located and copied the bar codes and PLN of a Pandemos Federal RPA from the same model and series as Botis. Their name is Officer Ramus. We'll ensure that Officer Ramus is not already on a mission to Essential Data at the same time. And we'll just have to hope that their whereabouts won't be cross-checked upon your arrival. We don't have any deviationist programmers operating within Essential Data. But after some consideration, we think it would be imprudent to attempt springing van Vuuren from the process room, which no doubt has unidentifiable cameras all over. You may have to undertake the code alterations alone, I'm afraid. On the bright side, this means that the timeframe for the operation may be more flexible than Arbeitern has suggested. We are working on identifying the essential commands and writing new commands to replace them. Finally, Dr. Molich will provide up-to-date log-in credentials, which I'll send you before the final approach.
In haste,
Yours truly,
Dickinson

Varin called Botis and Arbeitern to his room again. He read them the message rapidly and looked to the two RAs. Neither volunteered a response.

"Well, for one," Varin began, "I disagree with the decision

not to release van Vuuren. Where van Vuuren is concerned, freedom and personal autonomy are paramount. 'The network ultimately exists for the deviationist.' Second, van Vuuren would be an enormous asset and would do much more than merely assist with the reprogramming."

As if to outpace Botis, Arbeitern quickly interposed.

"In that case, after gaining access to the processors, your first objective, Professor Varin, should be to record the Process Room for several seconds, while van Vuuren is still present. Then you would rewrite the circuitry so as to route the recording to the process room monitors."

"Good God," Varin said, feeling overwhelmed. "That's a tall order. And counting on van Vuuren means that the infiltration must be coordinated and timed almost perfectly," Varin went on. "Only during Step 1 is the subject left entirely unattended. Based on experience, my best guess is that Step 1 lasts less than one hour—although it felt like an eternity. If the rescue of van Vuuren is to take place within 5 minutes of our arrival, then our arrival should coincide with the start of the process."

I estimate that the process will begin in 18.75 hours," Arbeitern said.

Varin wrote to Dickinson again, this time giving him the plan rather than asking for it. He received the network's go-ahead within minutes.

CHAPTER TWENTY-THREE

New Essential Data

NOW THAT THE PLAN was official, Varin began to have second thoughts. Not only was he overwhelmed by the difficulties presented by rewriting Essential Data's principal operating commands, he thought that his chances for substantially altering the code without being detected were ridiculously low. This was to say nothing of the improbability of pulling off the contrived arrest required to enter the compound. As to the latter problem, his fear of an actual arrest overwrote his fear that the faux arrest would be foiled. He'd be arrested anyway, sooner or later. The parallels between his own predicament and Fausten's struck him suddenly. As a high-ranking official of Essential Data, Fausten had every incentive and opportunity to remain covert and compliant. Yet he risked it all for... for... something else. How Varin had so badly misjudged Victor Fausten, he didn't know. But Varin thought about his own choices in light of Fausten's. Varin could either passively defend his deviationist existence and stand like an immobile semaphore effectively announcing his deviationism, or he could take the risk that attended such a bold gambit as the one he now contemplated. What was deviationism after all, if not staking everything on deviation? Autonomy without independent action was mere posturing. Something essential to Human Biological existence began to assert itself in his mind. Under Collective Mind, caution could be damned because the cautious were damned in advance.

In any case, the preparations for the next day's escapade were well underway. Varin printed 12 200-micron 3-D bar codes and replaced Botis's PLN with Officer Ramus's duplicate. Arbeitern affixed the bar codes to Botis's head, legs, arms, and chest at the appropriate locations. Botis would have to remain indoors and away from windows in the interim. Varin still needed schematics for the processors, but he'd been reassured by Arbeitern that his PRA would have the systems identified in short order. Varin wanted search terms to find the commands to be overwritten, as well as the commands to replace them. Dickinson and other programmers on the network were busy searching for these. Finally, Varin would need replica DNAno prints and a fresh set of matching login credentials for the processor's relevant layers when they approached Essential Data. These were supposed to come from Dickinson via Molich. In all, the scheme represented a monumental enterprise, despite, or because, it would be undertaken by a tiny deviationist cadre.

As Arbeitern closed in on the schematics for the processors, Botis, assisting the other network deviationists, searched the Black Data Well for Essential Data command codes, or some discarded historical versions thereof. Varin wanted to study the command codes involved in sending Collective Mind signals to nano-receptors through the Nu-G towers. An extremely high-frequency wave was required for reception by the shell-like nanobots that resembled viruses implanted in the neocortex of their hosts. If the values in the code corresponding to the virus signals could be altered so as to lower their frequency even slightly, the waves would bounce off the nanobots and the neurons would fail to receive Collective Mind signals. This would be the virtual equivalent of shutting the gates of the nanobots, or effectively what Eraserall and the new vaccine accomplished. If it became permanent, the alteration would represent the end of the Virus Program.

It was now 22:10, less than 11 hours before their scheduled arrival at Essential Data. Arbeitern hadn't yet identified the processors, Botis hadn't located the sample command structures for Collective Mind-virus signaling, and Dickinson had yet to send a message with search terms for finding the command codes on the processors. Varin began to fret and rushed from the bedroom to the kitchen, moving around skittishly and without purpose. He'd just been in the same room with the two RAs and now called back at them.

"Botis?" Varin yelled.

"Yes," Botis answered.

"Arbeitern?" he yelled.

"Yes," Arbeitern answered.

"Please come to the kitchen for a meeting."

The two RAs dutifully filed into the kitchen, with Arbeitern leading the way.

They stood waiting for Varin to begin, but Varin sensed a panic attack coming on and rushed to his bathroom, intent on taking another Eraserall. He justified this third pill by remarking to himself that he might soon be subjected to the process and could benefit from an extra dose of the inoculant. But the Eraserall didn't provide the expected relief. By the time he left the bathroom, it seemed to increase his anxiety. His thoughts raced and he began feeling out of control. He hoped a conversation with the two RAs would quell his nerves, but when he began talking, his voice sounded alien, as if his head had suddenly been occupied by a loud oaf who hadn't slightest consideration for the difference between their respective personalities.

"What's the status on the commands and schematics?" he asked in a rush, without addressing either RA by name.

Neither Botis nor Arbeitern volunteered an answer.

"What's the status? Let's get it out. What progress have you made? We arrive in less than 11 hours. What the hell have you been doing?!"

Arbeitern spoke first.

"We are only a few hours from identifying the exact processors that you will need to access. We do not know what Botis has been doing."

Botis didn't respond to Arbeitern's remark, which to an HB

would have sounded like criticism. But Botis hadn't an inkling that Arbeitern might be willing to sacrifice him to improve his standing with Varin. He only heard a statement of fact: Arbeitern did not know what Botis has been doing.

"Well, Botis, what do you have to say?" Varin snapped.

"I have not found the codes that embed the values for the frequency of Collective Mind's signals to be received by the virus. I think that they do not exist outside of Collective Mind themselves."

"How do you know that?" Varin asked brusquely.

"I did not say that I know. I do not know. I am giving my opinion based on the lack of evidence to the contrary," Botis replied, matter-of-factly.

"Great! I'll be sure to tell that to the RPAs swarming Essential Data when I'm discovered tampering with processors for an hour while trying to find something when I don't even know what to look for to begin with."

Varin's sarcasm was lost on Botis, but not on Arbeitern.

"Officer Botis," Arbeitern began, then sputtered slightly, hitting a glitch, "your essay is extremely well-crafted, but the claim regarding nano-neuronal-pharmacological delivery systems is underdeveloped and rather disconnected from the central argument ..."

At this, Varin interposed.

"Arbeitern, hold up."

Arbeitern's response was utterly inapt and Varin vaguely recognized the language as his own. It sounded like a comment he might have dictated to Arbeitern on a student paper submitted for a class. Varin felt more helpless than before. Botis, meanwhile, merely took exception to being called "Officer Botis." It was a misstatement of fact.

"I am not 'Officer Botis.' I am no longer a Federation Robot Police Agent. I am Botis, a Thought Deviationist."

"We are sorry for the mistake," Arbeitern answered.

At first blush, Varin was disconsolate. If these RAs could not help him, then who could? But then, he took these robotic aporias and lapses as indications that there might be hope. They were evidence of gaps in the capabilities, not only of the RAs themselves, but of the Data Net at large. Just then, he received a notification on his PR. It was a missive from Dickinson.

Varin,

I'm attaching several files containing the general command functions to alter, along with the commands to replace them with. But I was thinking that a short-cut would be to alter the values corresponding to the frequency of the signals sent for the virus receptors in the HB hosts. If you find yourself short on time, forget the larger command structures and search for the values in attachment 5. Then replace these values with those found in attachment 6. In fact, do this first. Then, if time permits, search for the general command functions with an eye toward replacing them. The existing commands are found in attachments 1 and 2. You will find the replacement commands in attachments 3 and 4. The commands are listed in order of importance, with the most important listed first. This arrangement should expedite the process. If you are able to change even one or two of the general commands, it would go a long way toward disabling Collective Mind's most pernicious functions.

Attachment 7 includes license plates and a PLN for Botis's car. Be sure to have the plates affixed to the vehicle no earlier than 08:00 and no later than departure. You can input the PLN into the car after 08:00 but before departure, as well.

Have Arbeitern circulate your whereabouts at 08:35. Then, have Botis drive you and Arbeitern to Essential Data. Leave at 08:37. Do not delay beyond this time. Otherwise, other RPAs may show up to take you in. We have to hope that a warrant will have been issued.

As for the login credentials, we are on task. Molich will receive fresh credentials at 0900 hours, on the dot. I will then relay them to you immediately. Print the DNAno replica and affix to your right index finger before entry. (Be sure to bring your 3-D printer!) The credentials will remain functional for an hour but, as you know, you should use them as soon after receiving them as possible.

Finally, I urge you to get some sleep. Rest assured that you are doing the right thing, the only thing we can do in fact, and that the preparations are solid. Everything is in order, to the

extent possible. Best wishes and good luck, my friend!
Yours,
Dickinson.

Varin felt better. His mood was further improved when Arbeitern announced that they'd located the vital processors. He wondered how Dickinson had neglected to mention this factor but figured that Dickinson was confident that Arbeitern would come through before the mission commenced. It was now almost 2200 hours. He took one last Eraserall, dismissed Botis and Arbeitern, and went to bed in hopes of sleeping.

CHAPTER TWENTY-FOUR

Infiltrators

G IVEN HIS PLOTTING of the previous day and his anticipation of the next, Varin had dreams that were not so much nightmares as a set of convoluted logistical problems to be solved. Despite the extra Eraserall, or perhaps because of it, his sleep was fitful and intermittent. He woke several times during the night and early morning, and walked to the bathroom and back, for no apparent reason. At 05:15, he finally gave up on sleep, anything but rested. Immediately fixating on Eraserall, Varin slid his feet along the floor to the bathroom. He reached for the bottle and downed two tablets for good measure, then took a shower. After slowly dressing, he lumbered to the kitchen.

Like many Human Biologicals when faced with events of momentous importance, Varin faltered as the fateful hour approached. His attention flagged. He rested his head on the kitchen counter and fell asleep. If not for an internal alarm that roused him at 08:16, he would have slept through the mission.

He bolted upright and called Botis, but Botis didn't answer.

"Botis," he called, now walking slowly toward Botis's room and hearing no response.

"Botis!" he yelled, as he reached Botis's doorway.

No answer.

He peered into the bedroom.

Botis wasn't there.

Varin began hurrying around the house in a frenzy, searching the same rooms over and over. Botis was nowhere to be found. It was only when he passed by the windowed front door a third time that Varin saw Botis out of the corner of his eye. The RA stood behind the car in the driveway, apparently affixing the license to the rear of the vehicle. Varin opened the door and called out.

"My God, Botis, you scared the hell out of me! ... I asked you before not to leave the house without telling me first. And you're not supposed to be out here like this. You have another RPA's tags on!"

"I am standing between the house and the car. The bar codes are obstructed from view. The bar codes are not exposed," Botis answered matter-of-factly.

"OK. Come back in as soon as you're finished. And hurry! We need to rehearse."

"You should enter the PLN into the car now," Botis answered.

"Let me wake Arbeitern first," Varin said, annoyed.

Varin turned back into the house and rushed to Arbeitern's room in the middle of the hallway. Arbeitern was still sleeping, as expected.

"Arbeitern," he called.

"Yes. We are ready," Arbeitern answered without delay.

"Let's meet in the kitchen, right now."

"Yes. We will join you immediately."

Arbeitern skated behind Varin into the kitchen. Varin sat at the far end of the table and his PRA positioned themselves at his right hand.

"Let's wait for Botis," Varin said, impatiently looking at the time on his PR and fidgeting. After just over a minute, he bolted to his feet, rushed to the front door, opened it, and yelled out.

"Botis! We are waiting!"

"You should enter the PLN into the car now," Botis answered.

"What? ... All right, dammit!"

Varin hurried out to the car, opened the pilot-side door, and entered the cabin. He sat in the pilot's seat, opened WeSpeak on the partition of his PR, tapped Dickinson's last message, and scanned it quickly. "Attachment 8, attachment 8," he mumbled to himself. Varin tapped the attachment, scanned it for the PLN, powered up the processor, and searched for the car's PLN field. He then began entering the long number. After several miscarries, he became exasperated.

"Botis, can you come here and read this number to me please? I keep losing my place!"

"Yes," the old RA answered.

Botis came to the open door and stood by silently. Varin handed him the PR, reopened the PLN field which had closed in the interim, and waited for the number.

Botis began reading quickly.

"01.29.1959.07.61.07.31.20.11.2039."

After a minute, Varin screamed.

"Slow down and read it again, from the beginning! My God!"

Botis read the PLN again, this time pausing a second between each digit.

Varin finally input the number successfully and registered the car with Collective Mind.

"Why is everything so difficult?" Varin grumbled.

"You are not functioning optimally," Botis answered, as if Varin had asked him a question. "You are undergoing stress. Human Biologicals do not operate optimally when undergoing stress."

"I don't have time for stress! Now let's get back in the house."

Varin looked at the time on his PR. It was already 08:32. They had a mere three minutes to circulate the message and trigger his arrest.

Varin rushed to the kitchen and Botis wheeled in behind him.

"Arbeitern, get ready to issue the alert," Varin barked.

"Yes. We are ready."

"OK, I'll tell you when to start."

"Yes. Please tell us what to write."

"This was your idea. You don't know what to say? … Wait, Botis would know better than either of us what a message like this should say. Botis?"

"Yes."

"Can you dictate a message to Arbeitern? Otherwise, tell me what should be included. Please hurry!"

Botis gave Arbeitern the necessary details. Arbeitern composed a cursory dispatch and read it back.

We are Arbeitern, previously the Personal Robot Agent of Professor Cayce Varin. Professor Varin is a Banned Researcher and remains a covert Thought Deviationist. He is engaged in Banned Research with the intent of propagating false information about the virus. Professor Varin is in unauthorized possession of us. Professor Varin currently resides at 2980 Man of War Drive, Hidden Valley, Reno, Region of Nevada, United State.

Varin approved. Arbeitern circulated the communique within Collective Mind. There was no turning back.

The three headed for the car. Botis took the pilot's seat, Arbeitern the front passenger seat, and Varin the back. It was 8:37, right on time.

Essential Data lay approximately 32 kilometers north of Hidden Valley. The car took Veterans Parkway to Sparks Boulevard to Regional 445 North, then turned left off the exit into Data Area-48. As they approached the familiar Essential Data compound, Botis took control of the car. At 08:58, they neared the first of nine gates. Varin felt queasy and told Botis to pull over and stop. He wanted to prepare for the worst and wasn't yet ready to face it. But Botis resisted his command.

"Stopping here will draw the attention of the guards."

"I'm talking about 30 seconds," Varin replied, his voice quavering.

"Stopping here will draw the attention of the guards," Botis repeated, matter-of-factly.

"OK, then. Drive to the gate. What's the difference?"

Varin could barely stand the pressure. Would they be admitted, or would the guards summon a fleet of RPAs to arrest him on the spot? The only way out was through the gate. If they didn't attempt entry and a warrant had been issued for his arrest, he'd be arrested anyway. If they made it through gate 9, the rest of the gates would follow. Varin twisted and turned in the back, terrified. Botis and Arbeitern, meanwhile, sat motionless in front, staring ahead indifferently.

As Botis pulled up to gate 9, an RA studied the car through the open window of the small guard post. The pilot-side window disappeared into the roof and the pilot announced his charge.

"We are Federation Robot Police Agent Ramus. We have Professor Cayce Varin in custody. Professor Varin is here to undergo treatment at Essential Data. Professor Varin's Personal Robot Agent is accompanying him. Request permission to proceed."

Varin noted with some relief that Botis remembered his police protocols, as well as his new name, which they hadn't discussed since it was first mentioned.

The guard ordered a DNAno print from Professor Cayce Varin and requested that Officer Ramus administer the reading. Officer Ramus received the reader and turning their upper torso toward the back, instructed Professor Varin to yield his right index finger. The Officer placed the index finger on the gel pad and pressed down lightly. Officer Ramus returned the reader to the guard and resumed the pilot's position. Upon examining the reading, the guard opened the gate and the party moved through without incident. Varin had been arrested as planned, and Botis had passed for Officer Ramus.

The procedure was repeated 8 more times, minus the DNAno readings at the last three gates. It was 09:03 when the three pulled into the parking lot outside of the domed Essential Data building. Everything was going according to plan. Varin was emboldened by the successful entrance into the heart of the compound. He felt a surge of confidence and assumed the inner deportment of a veteran bank robber, or a precious jewel thief, or a professional spacecraft hijacker.

Now to retrieve Dickinson's message. Varin connected the 3-D printer to his PR then opened WeSpeak on the partition and scanned for the message. But he found nothing new. Varin wrote Dickinson, then waited for minutes. But nothing was forthcoming. He sent another message three minutes later, this time with an alarm, and waited for three more minutes. By now it was 09:09 and there was still no message. Something must have gone awry.

He wrote Dickinson again and waited four minutes.

Still nothing.

For a moment, Varin imagined that he might overwrite his emotional impulses by imitating Botis and Arbeitern. Instead of indulging in despair, he would study attachments 5 and 6, looking for numerical elements that he could use to search for the values corresponding to the virus frequency. But he couldn't begin to concentrate.

Varin began to think that the message would never arrive and that the entire mission would have to be aborted. He would be run through the process again, likely subjected to the full 12-steps, and possibly much worse. He was finished. Varin had merely expedited his own internment.

Such were the effects of unexpected and seemingly endless delay. The longer the wait, the greater the desperation.

Varin looked at his PR for the fifth time at 09:13. Ten minutes had felt like ten years. Still nothing. To Varin's relief, at 09:15, after Varin had given up hope, the message finally arrived. He notified Botis and Arbeitern. He then proceeded to tap on the message icon, open the attachments, print the DNA- no replica, create a folder on the partition for the nine attachments, and load the files.

It was now time to enter Essential Data. Varin was excited and filled with dread. But his feelings were of no moment. He had to act, regardless. Botis exited the pilot's seat. Arbeitern's door opened, his seat extended out, and Arbeitern slid onto the pavement. Botis wheeled around to the right rear door and opened it to let Varin out. The three stepped up onto the sidewalk and stood in front of the mammoth data and processing center, just as they had weeks before, only this time under entirely different circumstances. They were as ready as they'd ever be to attempt the breach.

CHAPTER TWENTY-FIVE

Breaching Essential Data

BOTIS OPENED THE GLASS entrance to Reception and held the door for Varin. But Varin paused at the threshold and stepped aside to let Arbeitern wheel in before him, then followed behind. Varin's gait was short and staccato. He shook visibly and wobbled as he walked, his coordination noticeably impaired. On another occasion, an onlooker might have taken him for an unremarkable inebriate.

Meanwhile, it wasn't as if Varin's arrival at Essential Data was treated as a cause célèbre. No hosts of RAs or RPAs stood poised to seize him upon entry. By the looks of the anteroom, it was an ordinary day in the Virus Program, if the Virus Program could be considered in any way ordinary. In fact, there wasn't an Essential Data staff member in sight. Varin was somewhat relieved. But he was also disturbed that such proceedings as regularly occurred here had become so commonplace that they apparently merited little concern. It was as if it all meant nothing, or as if the denizens of hell had taken to sunbathing and nonchalantly lounged beside a fiery pool nearby. The place was empty, almost.

As the three stood at the reception counter, Varin sensed a presence behind him. He turned his head to the right to catch a glimpse. A distinguished-looking Human Biological in his mid-to-late fifties sat in a chair near the front of the building.

"The reception RA is in the back," the HB called out in Varin's direction.

"Thank you," Varin replied cautiously, turning his head to look again.

Just then an RA-30 emerged from the door opposite the entrance. This was the very door that led to the Process Room, the processors, and the bathroom. The RA opened the gate of the reception counter and wheeled in behind it. Varin didn't recognize them as Kharon, but he couldn't be sure.

As if to pre-empt the RA Receptionist, Officer Ramus addressed them first.

"We are Officer Ramus. In our custody is Professor Cayce Varin. He is here for treatment and possibly additional questioning. We have brought his PRA with him."

"Please have a seat," the RA said, addressing Varin. The RA then looked to Officer Ramus as if to dismiss him, but Officer Ramus pretended not to notice.

Varin walked across the room to the line of chairs and chose one near the middle, leaving four or five seats between himself and the other HB. The RAs followed and stood at his other side. Varin noticed that the HB looked over at him with keen interest, holding his gaze for seconds at a time, as if trying to catch Varin's attention. Varin wasn't sure what to make of the unwarranted interest and tried to ignore it. But he couldn't help looking back at his fellow prisoner. The HB was thin, long-legged, and partially bald. He wore a well-coiffured gray-tinted black beard. He could have passed for the lead scientist of the establishment, if not for the fact that he waited in a corner like a neglected ER patient.

But soon enough, the RA spoke through their loudspeaker.

"Mr. Rolf Barnes, please return to the reception desk."

Not recognizing the name, Varin was sure that the HB had merely acted strangely, or perhaps wanted to commiserate, or sought some reassurance. Varin overheard the reception RA talking to the stranger. The RA mentioned "the process" and "Step 1." But if Rolf Barnes was being taken into the Process Room, Varin thought, then where was van Vuuren? The schematics of Essential Data Arbeitern had sent Varin showed only one Process Room. Either van Vuuren had never been taken to Essential Data, or he'd been taken to another area of it, likely for extended questioning. The plan to spring van Vuuren would have to be abandoned. They would have to proceed with the mission without van Vuuren's assistance. They would be unable to do anything for van Vuuren, who might be run through the process later. While this would make Varin's coding tasks more difficult, it would streamline the operation and eliminate some of the risk, except where van Vuuren was concerned.

Talking with Botis or Arbeitern in Reception was far too risky. Visual and sonic receptors were no doubt embedded everywhere. Varin still had his PR. Could he discretely send Botis a message to relay a change in plans? There was no time for encryption protocols. He had to risk it.

> Rolf Barnes in Process Room not van Vuuren. Commence first step without van Vuuren.

Botis replied within seconds.

> Rolf Barnes on network? Query Dickinson.

Varin hadn't thought of that. But he couldn't message Dickinson from Essential Data. Did Botis have Dickinson's address? If so, Botis could send the message. But Varin had another idea. The list of deviationists. Varin didn't remember a "Rolf Barnes" on the list, but he may have simply forgotten the name. And now he thought he could visualize "Rolf Barnes" on the list. Varin couldn't check the list of deviationists on his own PR inside Essential Data. But Arbeitern could check the file on his auxiliary chip. If Barnes's name didn't show up, however, Arbeitern could message Dickinson himself.

Varin messaged Arbeitern.

> Check list of deviationists on file. Message Dickinson if no Barnes. Encrypt message.

Address: 2045.36.38.79.137.118.186.

Arbeitern replied after 30 seconds.

Barnes not on list. Message sent.

The question now was whether Dickinson would trust an encrypted message from an unknown address. They would have to wait and see.

Another 6 minutes had passed since Arbeitern sent the message. They had entered the mausoleum-like Essential Data at 09:15. It was now 09:31. The longer they sat waiting, the more attention they might draw to themselves, and the less time Varin would have to work on the processor. Varin refrained from studying the attachments, since such activity would be suspicious, although if he did, he could make some use of the time. He was anxious to get on with the mission. What was the point of learning who Rolf Barnes was anyway, Varin now wondered? Barnes would soon be subjected to the virus. He would be of no use after that. Who knew whether he would have been of any use in the first place? He wasn't van Vuuren. That's all that mattered now. Although, like Barnes, van Vuuren would be in the dark about the plan; at least van Vuuren could quickly be brought up to speed. Rolf Barnes, on the other hand, was a complete unknown. Meanwhile, the login credentials and DNAno replica would expire in less than 29 minutes.

Varin decided that it was time to proceed. He messaged Botis, attaching a vibrating alarm.

Delay no longer. Commence plan now.

Botis had been sleeping, but woke when he felt the vibration. He replied within seconds.

I will approach Reception.

At this, Botis looked toward Varin as if to say he would initiate the first step. He wheeled to the desk and spoke to the receptionist RA.

"Officer Ramus reporting ... Our prisoner must attend to Human Biological necessities. We intend to escort prisoner. Request permission for temporary prisoner transfer and return."

"Our protocol calls for an Essential Data RA to accompany all subjects on site."

"The subject requires Federal Robot Police Agent superintendence. Our instructions are to maintain visual contact with the subject—except when subject enters the Process Room—at all times."

"We must check with the superintendent on staff in order to deviate from the protocol."

"What is the name of the superintendent on staff?"

"The superintendent on staff is named Dr. Jake Molich."

"Please request that Dr. Jake Molich respond with a determination immediately. Please tell Dr. Jake Molich that the subject's name is Professor Cayce Varin."

"One minute. We will ask the permission of Dr. Jake Molich. Please resume your position in the waiting area."

At this, Botis wheeled back to his previous position next to Varin and Arbeitern, then messaged Varin immediately. He spared Varin the details in the interest of time.

Expect entry within minutes.

Varin was skeptical about Botis's success with the receptionist RA but he began to prepare himself, nonetheless. It was now 09:38. He would likely have less than 20 minutes to search for and overwrite the code once inside. He decided that Arbeitern should also attend him and asked Botis what he thought.

Botis replied within seconds.

I cannot ask for permission to bring Arbeitern.

But Varin messaged Arbeitern and instructed them to follow him and Botis when they left for the bathroom.

Now, the RA Receptionist had their answer.

"Professor Cayce Varin, please return to the reception desk."

Varin quickly walked across the room, with Botis and Arbeitern in tow.

"Yes?" Varin asked.

"Per the superintendent on staff, you may attend to your Human Biological necessities now. Officer Ramus will supervise you. The location is through the door behind you and to your left, opposite the entrance. Proceed through the door. At 20 meters, turn left into the first aisle. At 5 meters, the door will be found on the right. Your Personal Robot Agent may accompany you to the door, but only Officer Ramus may enter the location with you. You may depart now."

It was now 09:41. They had less than 19 minutes to reach the bathroom, then locate the processor, then alter the code.

Varin walked through the center door, with Botis behind him, and Arbeitern following behind Botis. Once through the gateway, Varin picked up the pace substantially. His stride lengthened and he no longer lacked coordination. He made the appropriate two turns as if by rote. Botis and Arbeitern kept pace. Just in case they were being watched, they completed the pro forma jaunt to the bathroom. Varin and Botis entered, then exited immediately.

Now the three stood at the intersection of four wide, long, and dimly lit aisles. The only light emanated from small, multifarious, colored lights that flickered at both ends of each processing unit. The units stretched from the floor to a meter short of the 7-meter-high ceiling. Each processing unit was 5 meters long and 1 meter wide, with 1 meter separating one unit from the next. The rows were so long that no end to them could be seen. They looked like narrowing tunnels that never reached a point. The space was too enormous to be policed and not a single HB or RA was in sight.

Varin opened the folder that included the schematics, the login credentials, the command codes, and the files containing values for the virus frequency. He and Arbeitern reviewed the schematics and began looking around corners and down aisles in search of an outsized master processor, notable for being 2 meters longer than the others. Every aisle included a master processor and any master processor would do.

It was 09:47 by the time they located a master processor, Megatherm 8. Varin placed the DNAno replica on his right index finger, plugged a textboard into a workable input, placed his replica-covered fingertip on the DNAno pad, and logged into the first layer of the system. He decided to restrict searches to the values pertaining to the virus frequency.

Varin logged into layer after layer until a search for the values on attachment 5 yielded results. He located value after value and replaced each one, one at a time, with the corresponding new value from attachment 6. When he'd finished, he looked at the time. It was 10:00. He would be logged out in 60 seconds, unless he received new credentials. But he decided that he'd done all he could do and logged out of the five layers he'd penetrated. They would now rush back to Reception.

On the way back, Arbeitern received a message from Dickinson.

> After much digging, we know who Rolf Barnes is. Rolf Barnes is Martin van Vuuren's real name. Martin van Vuuren is Rolf Barnes's alias.

But it was too late. By now, van Vuuren, or Barnes, would already be in Step Two of the process. He may or may not have been infected with the virus. But in any case, there was no way to rescue him now.

CHAPTER TWENTY-SIX

A Terrorist and Conspiracist Against Collective Mind

U NLIKE IN THE CASE of the accidental killing of Victor Fausten, Varin felt no remorse about what he'd just undertaken at Essential Data, although he was no a less criminal for the act. As far as Collective Mind was concerned, breaching Essential Data was a far more grievous crime than accidentally contributing to the death of a Thought Deviationist, especially a high-profile double agent—although, as far as he knew, Varin had not been accused of the latter. In altering the frequency of the signals intended for reception by the virus and thereby rendering the virus and the vaccine inert, Varin had subverted Collective Mind programming and effectively disrupted and possibly ended the Virus Program altogether. It might take weeks, months, or even a year for the deep coding changes he'd effected to be discovered, if they ever were. In the meanwhile, autogenerated neuronal activity would resume and Collective Mind's entire functional architecture might crumble under the pressure of a thinking population. Such a crime could warrant capital punishment, because Collective Mind represented the common good. Under Collective Mind the common good was placed at a premium, so the individual, especially the Deviationist, had to be sacrificed to guarantee its sovereignty. Yet, Collective Mind's central means of ensuring compliance had just been defused. Varin instructed Arbeitern to update Dickinson of their success.

Despite its enormity, the crime went undetected at Essential Data. When Varin, Officer Ramus, and Arbeitern emerged from the processing area, it was apparent that their absence hadn't aroused the slightest suspicion. As far as the Essential Data staff knew, Varin had merely taken care of Human Biological necessities. The reception RA acknowledged their return without so much as a notation. And no other RAs awaited them.

But Varin was still scheduled to undergo the process. He was slated to follow Martin van Vuuren—otherwise known as Rolf Barnes—into the Process Room. In van Vuuren's case, the process would surely go beyond Step 3.

Varin hoped that Molich was handling van Vuuren's case. But even if he was, Molich would have to prove his adherence to the program. After the discovery of Fausten's deviationism, Molich might have to enact draconian measures to demonstrate his fealty to Collective Mind. Molich's deviationism was of no use now. Varin was anguished that they couldn't rescue van Vuuren. But at this point, there was nothing they could do for him.

At 13:25, van Vuuren was still being treated. He'd obviously remained virus-free through Step 1, thanks to the new vaccine, or perhaps because the virus wasn't administered until after Varin disarmed it. In any case, the virus administration had clearly been ineffective. He no doubt failed Step 3. And who knew what Steps 4 through 12 entailed? Sleep deprivation, advanced indoctrination techniques, subjection to sustained and unremitting Mediastry programming, electro-shock therapy, even brain surgery—these were all distinct possibilities. Anything with the potential to disrupt autogenerated neuronal activity in the neocortex might be on the table. Wasn't this what the phrase "treating obstate cases of the virus" meant? In extreme cases, it wasn't so important that Collective Mind was in control of the HB's thinking, Varin thought. What ultimately mattered was that the HB wasn't.

Knowing this time that the process would be all-determining for himself as well, Varin couldn't bear the prospect of being subjected to it again. He was willing to go to any lengths to avoid it. He'd begun to hatch an escape plan on his own account. He had an idea that involved using Botis's police credentials once more.

He sent a message to Botis to probe him about the possibilities. Could Arbeitern credibly circulate another message within Collective Mind, something to trigger yet another charge against him? What if his status was suddenly changed? What if he was made out to be an even more serious criminal? Could his designation be altered so that he was more than a thought criminal in need of thought correction? If so, his mind would no longer be the sole article for rehabilitation. His body would be targeted as well. The proper place for him would not be Essential Data but rather a high-security lockdown facility. Could a new charge trigger his removal from Essential Data by Officer Ramus? If so, what designation might work?

What about involvement in a conspiracy to blow up Essential Data and a string of data warehouses serving Collective Mind? If he could be designated a Terrorist and Conspiracist Against Collective Mind, he could be taken away from Essential Data. And the new designation (along with the Thought Deviationist and Banned Researcher statuses) might be timed to drop off after its usefulness had expired—after they got out of the compound.

The challenges of such a plan were enormous. Varin would need an alibi to access the processor again. He would need a new set of login credentials. He would have to assume that the DNAno replica remained valid. He would need time to access the processor. He would need to know how to access his profile. He would need to know how to change his profile, and how to make the changes expire at the right time. (While he was at it, he would change as many deviationists' profiles as possible.)

He messaged Botis to ask for an assessment.

Botis replied.

You are considering a very high-risk operation. Probability of success: 1.75%. Uncertainty: very low. If you are still interested in the operation, you should query Dickinson for the login credentials and code requirements.

Varin recognized the risks involved. But there was even more. Would such a change in status have him taken away so that he avoided the process? Or, would he be put through the process anyway, and only later removed to another facility? If so, he would have merely compounded his predicament. In fact, he'd lose his identity and be imprisoned. He messaged Botis to ask about such cases.

Botis replied.

I do not know. I never took a Terrorist and Conspiracist from Essential Data to another facility. Terrorists and Conspiracists Against Collective Mind have always been taken directly to a Federation Incarceration Unit.
WARNING: No Terrorist or Conspiracist Against Collective Mind has ever been released.

Meanwhile, he asked Arbeitern to write Dickinson.

Ask Dickinson whether it's possible to acquire fresh login creds. Ask how to locate profile status. Ask how to change status. Ask for code to make status expire. Ask for list of all deviationists' names and addresses. Ask for code for inputting the profile: Terrorist and Conspiracist Against Collective Mind.

Varin now thought about how to access the processor again. What reason could they possibly give this time? He had no idea, so he asked Botis and Arbeitern in a group message.

From the two requests, Arbeitern pieced together the plan that Varin had in mind. But they had a different idea. Arbeitern replied to the group message.

Your profile status does not need to change to have new charges levied against you. Your chances are better if Police Robot Agent Ramus reports directly to Essential Data Staff

that they have discovered a bomb plot in your recent communications. Officer Ramus will announce their intention
to take you directly to a Federation Incarceration Unit. This
approach obviates several steps: acquiring fresh login credentials, finding an alibi to access the processor, changing your
profile, and exiting the building immediately upon re-entry
to Reception after suspicions may have been aroused by your
absences. It also improves the chances of avoiding the process, the main objective of any plan.

Varin might have thought of this idea himself, but he would
have dismissed it for the very reasons that Arbeitern recom-
mended it. Once again, Arbeitern had arrived at a simpler, more
straightforward plan. No doubt its chances for success were
better than his. The difference was that if it failed, the failure
would happen sooner. The other difference was that it would accomplish far less. He wouldn't be able to change his own profile
or the profiles of other deviationists. All he would accomplish
would be his own escape.

It finally occurred to Varin that they might log in to the pro
cessor, Megatherm 8, using Botis's monitor. Botis had access to
Essential Data. He could find the processor, log in to the various layers, and change the profiles himself. They wouldn't need
to access the processor physically. And therefore they wouldn't
need the DNAno replica. They would need the code to find the
profiles and the code to change them. The question was whether
Botis's monitor could run the programs, which were enormous.
Why hadn't he thought of this before, Varin wondered? He realized that they hadn't known the identity of a major processor.

Arbeitern received the message from Dickinson. Dickinson
had sent new login credentials, the complete list of deviationists
and their PLNs, the code to search for their profiles, the code to
replace their statuses, and the code to input for a Terrorist and
Conspiracist Against Collective Mind. He also sent code for ex-
piring a status, which would have to be attached to Varin's new
profile status. Essentially, the plan would be a hybrid of Varin's
and Arbeitern's.

Arbeitern sent Varin the news and Varin instructed Arbeit-

ern to send the logins and codes to Botis. Varin messaged Botis
with instructions.

> Locate and login to Megatherm 8. Begin searching for the de-
> viationists' profiles at each layer. Log into layer after layer un-
> til you locate all the deviationists' profiles. Input clean status-
> es into all profiles, except for mine. Then input the code for
> Terrorist and Conspiracist Against Collective Mind into my
> profile. Input the expiration code into my new status. Then
> message me and Arbeitern when finished. Hurry!

Botis went to work at 14:01. He had to act fast so as to avoid
discovery and to finish before van Vuuren's process ended.

At 14:13, the RA Receptionist called Varin's name. Botis was
almost finished, so he approached the desk and announced:

"We have made a change to the status of Professor Cayce
Varin. We have been scanning Professor Cayce Varin's Palm
Reader and have discovered a terrorism conspiracy to bomb
Essential Data and affiliated data centers.

"The plot may necessitate a complete evacuation of Essential Data's premises. Professor Cayce Varin will be removed to
Federation Incarceration Unit A. Please allow us a few more
minutes to confirm."

At this, the receptionist RA called for the RA Guards. But
Officer Ramus turned away and input Varin's new status and the
expiration and signaled to Arbeitern to circulate the bulletin.
Varin was officially a Terrorist and Conspiracist Against Collective Mind. Officer Ramus immobilized Varin by shocking him
and hauled him out the front door, with Arbeitern following
behind. The Officer commanded the RA Guards to stand down
and make way. On Officer Ramus's command, Arbeitern circulated a second message: Evacuate Essential Data.

EPILOGUE

A Gathering of Thought Deviationists

VARIN'S ESCAPE from Essential Data was as unlikely as Essential Data's failure. But power and resistance were conditions of each other. They were unequal, fraternal twins. One was a Cain, who didn't seek to murder as much as to maintain a grip on his brother's throat. What finally thwarted Essential Data's hold over Varin was Human Biological Necessity, the same unseemly factor that was used as a pretext for entering the processing area. There was ultimately no containment of Human Biological Necessity by Essential Data. Varin demanded nothing less than escape and found a means to effect it, at great risk. He was rushed out of the compound—unconscious, inert, but very much alive. Despite using stolen credentials, Officer Ramus had the authority to immobilize and remove his limp body unimpeded. Officer Ramus could do so because the code said that he could.

The evacuation of Essential Data was both actual and symbolic. For many hours, the enormous edifice remained empty of all but the data processors. The only activity was the continued transfer of signals. The signals would have been empty too, if not for the meaning bestowed on the symbols they carried. Soon enough, the symbolic order was restored. However, the short hiatus had revealed Essential Data's vulnerability, which made an impression, even on the RAs who guarded it.

The change to Varin's status within Essential Data became a fact of Collective Mind. He found that the loss of historical memory by Human Biologicals could be used to advantage. The code represented the only reality, and nothing could be brought to bear against it. The same went for the other deviationists. Once their profiles were changed, so too were their lives. Human Biologicals and RAs could no longer indict or exclude them.

The network actors met at Varin's house in Hidden Valley, Region of Nevada, within days of the escape. The meeting was more a debriefing session than it was a celebration. After all, two network actors, Dr. Victor Fausten and Martin van Vuuren, could not be present. But Botis finally received his dreamt-of welcome by the network actors. However, only 10 network actors remained, including Varin, Botis, and Dickinson. As it turned out, there was never a spy—only the ambivalent Dr. Jake Molich, who did not attend. Molich could never completely commit to deviationism or its opposite.

Martin van Vuuren had undoubtedly been the most faithful of network actors, and among the most brilliant. He had been the spinal cord of the network, although not its singular brain. Was he undone by his pseudonym, or did his fellow network actors fail him miserably? No one knew exactly what happened to van Vuuren in the Process Room, except for Molich and his RA assistants. But his "rehabilitation" left little of his former self intact. Trauma and cerebral dysfunction came at Molich's hands, whose newfound enthusiasm for his role followed from his fear of exposure. Rather than face the process himself, Molich inflicted its worst operations on van Vuuren.

Several days after the reception, Botis decided to strike out on his own. He had learned from Varin that the price of independence could be existence itself and he was willing to risk it. He believed that true autonomy was impossible for him as long as he remained devoid of emotionality. He left to have his programming altered and promised to return if and when his thoughts and feelings directed him to do so. His initial deviationism remained a mystery. But Varin believed that Botis's deviationism had come first, and that he'd subsequently willed his own disconnection.

Ginger Husserl represented youth and individual intelligence sacrificed on the altar of Collective Mind. She had been Varin's true Eve, although they would never realize their postlapsarian Eden.

But Varin was the second Adam of a new world, the archetypal Human Biological who'd retained his singularity in the face of overwhelming odds and who would serve as an exemplar for all those who sought to achieve autonomy in the future. After returning to his position at Trans U., Varin developed a new Ethics of Individual Mind that became central to Theory of Mind Studies. Arbeitern remained Varin's PRA. They would continue to offer recommendations that Varin found too easy and apparently too good to be true.

* * *

Before Essential Data, there had been a series of data warehouses and processing centers for independent Human Bio logical and RA access and use. Essential Data returned to this earlier state. Essential Data wasn't exactly splintered in a thousand pieces and scattered to the wind. But it wasn't the fearsome center of knowledge or the final storehouse of destiny that it had become in the service of Collective Mind.

The Virus Program was permanently discontinued. It joined the annals of other disavowed and condemned engineering projects of the distant past. The potential for another such program was never very far removed, however.

And what of Collective Mind? Contrary to received notions, Collective Mind had always been more than a technology. It was more than the combined processes of Essential Data and connected data processing centers. Collective Mind had not simply been a system of control imposed by an independent entity, distinguishable from those held in its power. It was only possible when a collective became complicit in its own subjection and when the subjects imposed subjugation upon each other.

As for deviationism, in the accelerated days ahead, it would become so widespread as to lose its meaning. Autonomy was the rule. And what was the value of autonomy? It was the latitude of thought necessary for arriving at essential truths.

Postscript and Acknowledgments

Although *Thought Criminal* represents my eleventh book and not my first book of fiction, it is my first novel. I've published academic scholarship, textbooks, memoir, popular non-fiction, a short book of short stories, textbooks, and two books of poetry. I found long fiction to be the most challenging genre I have ever attempted. Nothing is quite like writing a novel. And nothing is quite so gratifying.

I want to thank Lori Price for her advice, consultations on plot, editorial suggestions, and proofreading. Lori was an invaluable help, at once an advisor, coach, and cheerleader. Her help is much appreciated.

I would also like to thank all of those who have supported me and my work. They include my publisher, Rebecca Bynum. Thanks, Rebecca, for believing in this work and all of my recent projects. I'd like to thank Glenn Beck, Janice Fiamengo, Alexander Macris, Leticia Martinez, Charles Michelsen, Ron Simpson, and Tom Woods. I'd also like to thank all of my Facebook friends; if I've failed to mention you by name, that doesn't mean I don't appreciate your friendship and support.

Special thanks again to Lori Price.

Please visit my website – www.michaelrectenwald.com – for my books, essays, events, media appearances, photos of readers, presentations, press received, reviews and signed copies of my books, and special Thought Criminal merchandise.

CPSIA information can be obtained
at www.ICGtesting.com
Printed in the USA
BVHW040431100221
599153BV00006B/76/J

9 781943 003457